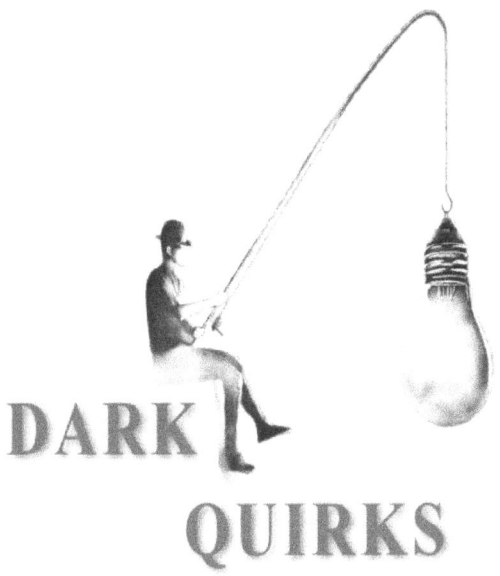

DARK QUIRKS

A COLLECTION OF SHORT STORIES

S. R. WEBSTER

DARK QUIRKS

First edition. August 1, 2025.

Copyright © 2025 S.R. Webster.

ISBN: 979-8991163934

Written by S.R. Webster.

Table of Contents

To all the indie authors who shatter barriers and redefine creativity with fearless abandon.

"You just have to trust your own madness."

Clive Barker

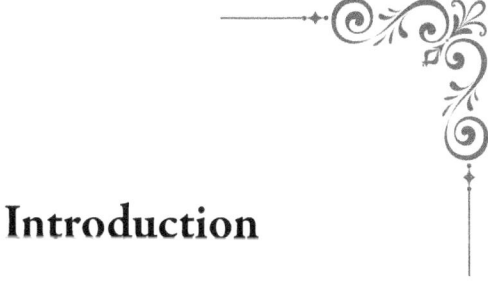

Introduction

Welcome to the eerie world of **Dark Quirks**! Brace yourself for a delightfully unnerving journey through this collection of previously published short stories, with a thrilling twist: within these pages, *The Uncanny Chronicles* makes its exclusive debut.

And if that's not enough to whet your appetite, there's a surprise bonus!

In a special, three-part collaborative piece, you'll be introduced to two remarkable guest authors, D. Lara Smith and Ellen Smith, who are surprisingly unrelated, despite sharing a surname. But resist the urge to skip ahead because these stories are arranged to mirror my publishing journey, which began in 2010 with my debut novel, *Butterfly Harvest*, an undertaking born of pure whimsy—or, more precisely, a haunting nightmare.

Many are familiar with night terrors, as most children experience them at some point in their early years and then typically outgrow them. But not everyone: for 4 percent of the population, those terrors persist into adulthood, and I am part of that group. Sometimes my dreams are so terrifying that I find myself waking not in my bed, but standing outside my room, screaming at nothing. Other times, I'm aware of my surroundings but completely unable to move. And then there are instances when I manage to escape the terrors by realizing I'm dreaming and soar high into the sky, fleeing the dangers below, well, most of the time. There have been moments when I could not escape the monsters. I've fallen, been shot, stabbed, bitten, burned, and more. These nightmares, in all their terrifying forms, have served as inspiration from the very start.

One morning, awoken by something I couldn't name and fueled by the fear that had plagued my restless night, I began writing fiction. I first wrote as a way to exorcise stress and past trauma. Before long, I discovered I was crafting a novel, and a fierce ambition took hold: finish it and share it with the world. However, when I decided to publish my first work (under the name Sandra R. Campbell), I encountered numerous obstacles. The path to publishing was far from clear, and there wasn't much guidance available at the time. Amazon had not yet become the publishing juggernaut it is today, and the environment for new authors was quite different. Traditional houses shied away from genre-bending work, such as mine, and self-publishing offered scant exposure and complicated distribution. Undeterred, I leaned into my rebellious streak, researching every option, networking with editors, cover designers, small presses, and other industry professionals until I carved out a comfortable niche in the writing community.

Since then, the term "indie author" entered our vocabulary, and with it came recognition for the creativity, effort, and dedication self-publishers pour into their work. Today, indie writers stand as pioneers forging their own paths in the literary world. Though I've tasted traditional publishing, I still relish the freedom and adventure of going indie.

In the past fifteen years, I've penned six novels, four of which—*Butterfly Harvest*, *Dark Migration*, *The Dead Days Journal*, and *A Girl Named Ghost* (my first as S. R. Webster)—have found their way into readers' hands. My early works were paranormal thrillers for younger audiences. As I grew, so did my interests, leaving two manuscripts incomplete and prompting a lengthy hiatus from writing. But the old adage "once a writer, always a writer" proved true. Eventually, my passion reignited, leading to my latest psychological thriller, *A Girl Named Ghost*, written for a more mature audience and published under a new pen name—my husband Greg's surname, which he's proud to see on the cover. Alongside these novels, many of my short stories have appeared in traditional venues, and you'll find several of them here. I've also included personal notes after each short, some highlighting the inspiration behind the stories, while others detail the creative processes and first publication credits. I hope these glimpses behind the scenes will deepen your enjoyment.

So, settle in, open your mind, and dive into the odd delights of ***Dark Quirks***!

Hands of Time

T he hand-crafted, chalet cuckoo clock hanging on the wall struck noon, triggering the squirrel to leap from his spot on the ledge as he did every day. And for the first time in eighty years, Ardit Kreshnik missed it. The old man should have been home hours ago.

On the worn workshop table, just below the clock, a scattered assortment of watchmaking tools lay abandoned: pinchers, key lots, magnifying glasses, a dust blower, and twenty or more tiny screwdrivers. Even Ardit's prized original German Steiner Jacot tool was left awry, which meant none of the small wheels, hinges, crystals, or bands would be assembled today. "Time won't keep itself," Ardit always said.

Several hours ticked away in the familiar rhythm of time, with each passing hour punctuated by the coo-calls from the weathered cuckoo bird's door. Finally, at six-fifteen in the evening, Ardit arrived home. Entering the cozy room in nothing but a blue hospital gown and a pair of chintzy slippers, Ardit dropped his crooked body into his tattered recliner, took one look at his beloved cuckoo clock, and closed his eyes.

"Quirrel, I didn't think I'd ever get out of there. That dense witchdoctor tried to keep me for good this time."

Your doctor's been trying to commit you for weeks. How'd you escape?

Ardit lifted his heavy lids to reveal two piss-shot, milky-grey eyes. He stared hard at his only friend in the world, an inanimate wooden squirrel. "I told the nurse I needed to stretch my legs. When the heifer wasn't looking, I ran down the back stairs and out the emergency exit."

"You ran?"

"Ran, hobbled, what's the difference?" Ardit laughed along with the squeaking giggles he heard in his head. "No one stopped me. I don't know why everyone insists I stay in the hospital when all I want is to be at home. People die alone every day."

At one time, Ardit knew the squirrel on his cuckoo clock didn't have the ability to talk, but many long, lonely years had softened his mind. The day his doctor diagnosed him with pancreatic cancer and informed him his life would end in months rather than years, Ardit muttered his anguished thoughts to an empty workshop. Only this time, there was a response. Quirrel announced his presence with a chirp and promised to accompany Ardit through the last days of his life.

When the sun rose the next morning, Ardit was still slumped over in his recliner, dreaming of a life he never took the time to live. Every waking hour of his adult years had been spent in his little house and workshop, ensuring time was kept. Kreshnik's watches were highly sought-after timepieces, famous all over the world, but Ardit had never taken a second for himself. Not for a wife, not for a family, not for friends. A hermit alone with his craft and his cuckoo.

"Ardit!" Quirrel cried out to wake his off-colored friend. As he continued to watch Ardit's restless sleep, he scanned

the contents of the workshop looking for a remote control to adjust the hue of Ardit's sickening color.

"Hey, Old Yeller, wake up! It's time to make the watch."

"Stop calling me that. I have liver failure. I'm not a dog." Ardit replied without opening his eyes and then shuddered violently with a series of uncontrollable hacks.

"Bark. Bark. Get to work, Old Man."

"That's better."

Ardit struggled to remove his narrow butt from the well-worn chair by rocking himself back and forth until he'd built up enough momentum to propel his fragile bones into a hunched, standing position. After an extended visit to the bathroom that was accompanied by several loud moans and a string of colorful curses, Ardit seated himself on a short stool in front of his precision-crafted, personalized worktable.

The hours passed slowly as Ardit worked nonstop on the ornate owl pocket watch. Some Hollywood big shot had contacted him with a high-paying, high-priority project. The quick-talking man had gone on and on about a great accomplishment by an actor in a blockbuster motion picture and an award ceremony for an Oscar something or other. But none of that mattered to Ardit.

It wasn't until the coos of noon chimed that Ardit paused to watch his friend Quirrel leap along the clock's ledge—lunch time. But Ardit couldn't eat anymore, not with the pain in his gut.

"Not eating lunch. Do you know you already skipped breakfast?"

"My stomach's a mess, besides, not much point in eating."

"I guess you're right. So, what happens when you finish the

watch?"

Ardit studied the empty, fine-brass casing and the metal-crafted owl eyes he'd designed, and decided they looked very wise. He was creating another collectible work of art and knew *this* watch would be loved above all others, because this would be his last.

"You know, you've spent most of your life keeping time, so why not make some instead?"

Reluctantly, Ardit lifted his eyes away from his work. "What do you mean?"

"If you reverse those wheel-gear thingies, you can get some time back and do the things you never had a chance to do."

"Quirrel, don't be ridiculous." Ardit rolled his shoulders once before reaching for his headlamp and securing the thick strap on his head.

"I'm not being ridiculous."

Ardit shot his wooden friend a nasty look. "Yes, you are."

"How do you know if you've never tried it?"

Ardit examined several of the wheels under his microscope, gazing into the idea of a possible future, and then shook the crazy notion out of his head. "Physics. That's how I know."

"What about me? Does physics explain why you spend all your time talking to a squirrel figurine on an old German clock?"

"I'm a sick old man."

"So, sick old man, do it. You're holding the gears in your hand. I know you're thinking about it. You're thinking about the what-ifs. What if I don't have to die? What if I feel better? What if I have the time to make a real friend? Come on, Ardit... what harm can it do?"

Ardit didn't speak to Quirrel for the rest of the day. He simply hunkered down to finish his work.

Night had fallen by the time Ardit was ready to test his handiwork. Methodically he wound the top knob counterclockwise, the spinning balance wheel tightly winding the spring. At last, it clicked. The watch was fully wound. Placing the clock on the worktable, Ardit stepped back and watched as the hands spun to life. Spinning so fast, he lost track of the tiny arms that were now only thin shadows speeding over the watch face.

"What did you do?"

"Only what you told me to do."

"Since when do you listen to me?"

"Hey, your color's back!"

"What?" Ardit ran to the small mirror hanging on the wall. The face looking back at him had vibrant grey eyes and wrinkle-free skin. No more jaundice. He was healthy and young. Very young. Ardit smacked his face and pinched his smooth forehead, just to make sure it was real.

"Impossible!"

A rapid knock at the door drew Ardit's attention away from his reflection. He moved quickly through the workshop, but when he reached the front door, he was too short to grab the handle.

"Quirrel, I'm a child!" Ardit squealed. "I have a whole life to live." Tears stung his round cherub cheeks.

The workshop door flew open, but Ardit couldn't see anyone or anything. It was so dark. Then a single pinprick of light appeared in the distance. The burning white orb expanded, growing bigger and moving fast toward the open door. Ardit tried to close it, but his infant hands were too small. He didn't have the strength to move it.

The light kept coming.

Ardit crawled under the table seeking protection. He yelled for Quirrel, though his fear had turned his words into indistinguishable sobs. And still the light came, flooding the workshop with blinding, white heat. Ardit's only escape was to close his eyes.

The next afternoon, the old cuckoo clock struck noon, and Quirrel leapt from his spot on the ledge, a familiar daily event that would continue to happen even though Ardit was no longer there to watch.

Author Note

I hope you liked *Hands of Time*. Before I published my second paranormal thriller, *Dark Migration*, I wrote my debut short story, which remains very dear to me. The protagonist, Ardit Kreshnik, is my most treasured creation so far. I initially crafted this story for *Waterfront Writers*, a fiction website that featured it in September 2013. This was my first attempt at speculative fiction, even though that wasn't my original goal. I usually overlook genre conventions because a good story stands on its own, no matter the category people try to fit it into. A story should develop naturally and become whatever it's meant to be. As I wrote this particular tale of woe, the setting and dialogue came to life vividly in my mind, much like a memorable scene from a favorite movie. The ending, although unplanned, was intentional, leaving it open for readers to determine Ardit's fate. Did the old watchmaker turn back time to live a life without regrets, or was it a hallucination brought on by death? Creative readers might even imagine an ending I hadn't thought of. In any case, I think *Hands of Time*

would make a perfect short for Pixar! Does anyone have their contact information?

Abandoned

In January 1985, my mother died in a car accident. Nobody's fault, just an accident. I think that's part of the reason my father couldn't handle it—couldn't handle me. There was no one to blame for her death.

Two horrible weeks later, my father crept through my doorway with a glass of wine in his hand to tell me I was no longer welcome. "Kate, you're going to stay with Uncle Jay for a while." His speech was slow and a little slurred.

A minute or two passed while I recovered from a sudden burst of fear, and then I babbled every question I had. "Why? When? How long? What do I need to pack?"

My father answered only one question before he turned and disappeared into the dark hall. "Pack everything."

The next day, we drove in silence to my uncle's house in upstate New York. The entire contents of my bedroom crammed into the back of my father's Jeep Cherokee. I can't say I minded too much. My uncle Jay was a professional football player—a Safety with the Buffalo Bills. He had a giant house I could get lost in, and a live-in maid to keep an eye on me, because I'm certain Uncle Jay would like an extra pair of eyes watching out for me. The best part was that I didn't have my sad-faced father lurking in shadowed doorways watching me when he thought I couldn't see.

The truth is, at sixteen, I looked a whole lot like my mother when they met in high school: pale skin, black hair, almond-shaped, stone-colored eyes. And just like her, I could make a color photo look black and white if the lighting was right. The eyes, though, that's what killed my father. He hadn't looked me in the face since the day of her funeral. Now, he wouldn't have to look at me at all.

Living with my rich and famous uncle turned out exactly as I expected. By April, I'd mastered the art of fake smiles and, for the most part, adjusted to my new celebrity lifestyle. Thanks to Uncle Jay, my abundance of superficial friends was never in short supply. He insisted I have people over almost every night; to study, eat pizza, watch a movie, or swim in the indoor pool. I had a feeling he didn't want to leave me alone for any length of time. Avoidance was Uncle Jay's way of dealing with his older sister's death. It wasn't mine, though. I wanted to talk about my mother, visit her grave, speak *to* her, but she was buried back home in our small-town cemetery, which happened to be more than a four-hour drive from Buffalo. No chance in hell Uncle Jay would lend me his Porsche to make that trip.

Surrounded by friends I didn't really want or need, and a new boyfriend, Luke, conveniently Bennett High's all-star quarterback, I abandoned the memory of my late mother in order to fit in. However, at some point, I realized my fabricated happiness had become something more. I'd forgotten how nice it was to smile without twitching or aching. My laughs weren't forced when Uncle Jay told me outlandish stories of his rookie year mishaps. Now his exaggerated tales brought pleasant tears to my eyes.

The night Luke presented his class ring and asked me to the senior prom, my heart pounded so hard I thought my ribs would crack—I did want to go. But as quickly as happiness returned to my life, it was gone again. A few days later, my father appeared, and every ounce of joy I had, vanished.

Saturday, May 11th, just after nine in the morning, Luke showed up in his fully restored '50s Ford truck and drove us out to Moosecup Lake for a day of sun, friends, and fun. We had the windows down, *And She Was*, by the Talking Heads, blared over the radio. Luke bobbed his head to the music while his arm inched along the back of the shiny bench seat.

"So, what's in the backpack?" Luke shouted over the music.

I tried not to smile when his thumb brushed the back of my neck but couldn't help the corners of my mouth from turning up. "I brought a book, a beach towel, a bag of chips, and a couple of sodas."

Luke's fingers trailed the curve of my shoulder and then dipped under the collar of my shirt. "What about your bikini?"

"The water's still too cold to swim," I said, removing his wandering hand from my shoulder and then entwining my fingers with his. Holding hands, hugs, and a few open-mouthed kisses at the end of a date was about as physical as Luke and I had gotten, and about as far as we were going to get.

We pulled onto the dirt road leading into Moosecup Lake behind a van full of kids from school. Luke honked his horn and waved as we parked next to them. Four guys from the football team and their girlfriends piled out of the van carrying backpacks and small coolers. I could smell the beer on them as soon as I got out of the truck. This wasn't the kind of fun

I had envisioned when Luke invited me to the lake. He and his friends didn't come to have fun, they came to party. So, the first chance I got, I slipped away with my backpack and started the two-mile hike down the main trail to the Moosecup Lake Welcome Center and a payphone.

Uncle Jay made sure I had a roll of quarters with me every time I left the house. Usually, I complained that they were heavy and weighed down my purse. But I was glad for it today. The first call rang busy, the second rang to infinity. The answering machine never picked up, and the stupid payphone kept eating the quarters it should have returned. I tried the house two more times but eventually gave up and called my uncle's pager. I entered the number of the payphone so he could call me back. I'd also added the numbers 9-2-2. Our private code meant it was important, but not an emergency. No need for him to panic, I wasn't in any danger. I only needed a ride home.

Ten minutes slipped away without a return call, and not another soul in sight. It was awfully quiet for a Welcome Center on a popular lake in the middle of spring. No park ranger, no volunteers, no visitors. I decided to suck it up and hit the trail back to Luke and his drunken posse.

When I reached the fork in the trail, my body tensed at the sound of loud punk music and obnoxious laughter. I'd been gone for over an hour, and I bet they hadn't even noticed. So, instead of heading to the Lake, I veered off the main trail to an eroded footpath with tricky rocks and fallen tree limbs. As soon as the noise faded, I felt my shoulders relax. It was a splendid kind of calm, with a gentle breeze through the thick trees and the faint rustling of dry leaves skittering over the ground. I'd planned to take the detour for just a few minutes. But then I spotted the dilapidated cemetery and tossed that plan out the window.

The overgrown and crumbling graveyard, and what looked like the decayed remains of a grey-brick church, lay forgotten in the middle of the woods. It was the perfect setting. I could talk to my mother here. Careful not to get pricked by the sticker bushes, I searched the broken and fallen headstones for the most legible epitaph for the next half hour. Most of the engravings were worn away by the harsh elements.

I'd almost given up when I discovered a corner of a weathered stone sticking out from under a clump of vines. Shoving the knotted plants aside, I saw the partially dislodged marker, pushed over by the expanding tree trunk, and the word 'Mother' clearly etched in the headstone.

Slinging the backpack from my shoulder, I removed a soda, popped the tab, and placed my backpack on the ground to use as a cushion. I had settled in front of the stone, preparing to unburden everything I wanted to say to my mother to a substitute grave, when a twig snapped behind me.

"There you are." A familiar voice I never expected to hear.

I jumped to my feet, spilling my Coke, and turned to see my father smiling. I'd forgotten what his crooked little grin looked like. "Dad, what are you doing here? How did you find me?"

My dad's smirk grew bigger with his front chipped tooth on full display. "Uncle Jay. And he won't be happy to hear about those boys drinking."

I wasn't sure how I felt about my father showing up. I thought I should be happy, but I couldn't say if I was or wasn't.

I'd pretty much written him off the day he decided to ditch me, considering him as dead as my mother. Still, I couldn't disappoint him. "Well, that's why I paged Uncle Jay, and also the reason I'm here and not there."

His eyes seemed to scan the woods behind me and then stopped, widening on a spot just over my left shoulder. "You always were a good girl."

I glanced back, but didn't see anyone or anything. "Gosh, Dad, you make it sound like that's a bad thing."

Swiping a shaky hand through his thinning hair, his eyes locked on mine. I watched his brown eyes fill with tears. "No, not bad. I'm the one who hasn't done right, not by you, and not by your mother. But I've come to make amends. Katherine, I'm sorry. I want you to come home. So, we can be a family again."

I took a long swig from my drink and swallowed. "Is that an apology? A few months ago, you couldn't even look at me. What changed?"

"Time is one of the reasons, and your mother's the other. She visited me recently, in a way that only the dead can. Now, when I talk to her, she listens. She answers. And I have a pretty good feeling that's why you're here in this old cemetery. You want to talk to your mother, too?"

"Yeah, I guess it is." He had never been more right about anything in his life.

My father reached forward with open hands but was still too far away to make contact. "Come with me. You can talk to her whenever you want. Your mother's come home to us. She's here to help us heal, to help us move on."

No more fake smiles, pretend boyfriends, or superficial friends. I could have my old life back. I could make peace with what happened to my mother and move ahead, my dad and I together as a family. Sure, I'd miss Uncle Jay. He and I were just starting to understand each other. Then again, it's not like I couldn't come back and visit. My father may have lost his wife, but I could give him back his daughter.

I snatched my backpack off the ground, slung it over one shoulder, and headed for the trail. "Okay, Dad."

"Don't you want to give me a hug?"

I turned around and saw my father standing scarecrow still, with his head down and arms stretched wide, waiting. He would frighten more than the crows standing like that. I wasn't about to run into those arms. Something felt off. Trust is a funny thing—once broken, it's always a little broken.

"I've gotta run back and tell Luke I'm leaving." With a jerk of my thumb, I indicated the direction of the lake. "It'll only take fifteen minutes. Do you want to come with me? Where'd you park the Jeep?"

My father took a couple of awkward steps toward me. His jerky, unnatural movements reminded me of a zombie flick.

Creepy.

I darted around the gravestones to the footpath and yelled back at him. "Meet me at the split in the trail."

When I finally reached the lake, I had shaken the uneasy feeling from the cemetery. It'd been silly for me to run away like that. My father showing up, out of the blue, while I was alone in the middle of an old graveyard, so we could talk about my dead mother was strange, but that was no reason to freak out. I'd let my overactive imagination get the better of me. Though I had to admit most of the afternoon had played out like an episode of *The Twilight Zone.*

Before I stepped off the trail and out of the woods, I heard yelling. "Where the hell is Kate?" I had a very upset uncle on my hands. Funny, my father said Uncle Jay would be mad to hear about the boys drinking. He hadn't said anything about my uncle being at the lake. Then again, Uncle Jay was probably the one who drove.

"Hey dude, back off. I can't help it if she ran off. I don't have a leash on the bitch—" Luke might have been a high school football stud, but he wasn't very bright. Lucky for him, I reached them before he finished his drunken, smartass reply.

"I'm here!"

I thought for sure I would be reprimanded right then and there, but instead, Uncle Jay's anger seemed to evaporate. Crushing me against his chest, he kissed the top of my head and then blew out a heavy sigh.

"Are you okay?"

It took me a second to maneuver around his iron grip so that I could look up. "Yeah, all good, Uncle Jay."

"Sorry, I didn't return your page right away. There was an emergency." Uncle Jay was already steering me towards the gravel parking lot. Passing Luke, he jabbed a stiff finger into his scrawny arm. "Kid, you better find another date for the prom."

The last thing I cared about was going to a stupid dance. "Is everything okay?" I asked as we were nearing the car.

Uncle Jay stopped. "No, honey, it's not."

When I turned around, I knew something had gone very wrong. But for the life of me, I couldn't conceive of anything that would make him cry. Well, maybe there was one thing. "Does it have anything to do with my father?"

Knuckling the tears from his face, he squared his shoulders

and took my hands in his. "Why would you ask that?"

"Because he's back on the trail waiting for me." Tears were building behind my eyes, threatening to flood over my mascara-coated lashes. I'd always hated to see a man cry.

My uncle's narrow eyes slowly grew wider. After a long silence, I thought he'd lost the ability to speak, but suddenly he dropped my hands and shouted. "That's impossible!"

"Uncle Jay, he's there. He said he came to take me home. He wants us to be a family again. I told him I'd go home. I thought you drove him here. You're not mad, are you, that I said I'd go?" I couldn't stop the tears from trickling down my face.

"Of course, I'm not mad that you'd want to go home with your father. The only problem is you can't." Uncle Jay reached out to swipe the tears from my cheek. The end of his finger came away smeared in black.

"Why can't I? Maybe we should go talk to him. He's waiting for me." I was scanning the woods behind him. My father was out there. He was waiting. And I had to go.

"No, he isn't."

"Seriously, Uncle Jay, he is." I pulled on his wrist, but it was like his feet were cemented to the ground. "I'll take you to him right now."

Uncle Jay grabbed my shoulders and gave me a hard shake. "Kate, your father's dead. He committed suicide early this morning."

"No!"

It's not true. It can't be true!

Wrenching free of my uncle's grasp, I ran into the woods. I had to see for myself that my father wasn't there. When I reached the fork in the main trail, I skidded to a stop. I could hardly believe my eyes. Standing two feet in front of me, in the center of the trail, was my slack-faced father in his frozen scarecrow stance, and beside him in the identical position was the decaying body of my dead mother.

"Katie." An unearthly voice seeped from my mother's brittle, barely moving lips. "It's time to come home."

Author Note

A *bandoned* was another story created for the same fiction website that published my debut short story. I drew inspiration from a random online photo of a neglected, overgrown cemetery. My approach to the story was a single question: What would a girl grieving the loss of a loved one do if she stumbled upon an abandoned graveyard? The story developed from there. The first publication received high praise, and it later appeared in the August 2015 issue of Suspense Magazine. After the second publication, I received a call from John Raab, Editor and CEO of Suspense Magazine. Chilling Entertainment had contacted him, expressing interest in adapting my story for their Simply Scary Podcast. Needless to say, I was excited at the opportunity to breathe new life into this eerie tale of loss.

Abandoned was featured on the Simply Scary Podcast in February 2017. Chilling Tales for Dark Nights, Season Two, Episode Two was hosted by G.M. Danielson, with performances by Olivia Steele as Kate, Marshall Regdale as

Luke, and Jesse Cornett as Uncle Jay. I was delighted with their rendition. Though it was odd at first to hear others speaking the words I had written and acting out the characters I had created.

My story also inspired the artwork for the website's episode, which was a surprise to me when it aired. I'm not quite sure how to describe the feeling I had when I first saw my words transformed into a haunting image, but I can say that it was beyond gratifying. So, a big shout-out to the artist, David Romero, for that! To see his artwork or listen to the podcast, go to simplyscarypodcast.com and search under the category Chilling Tales for Dark Nights.

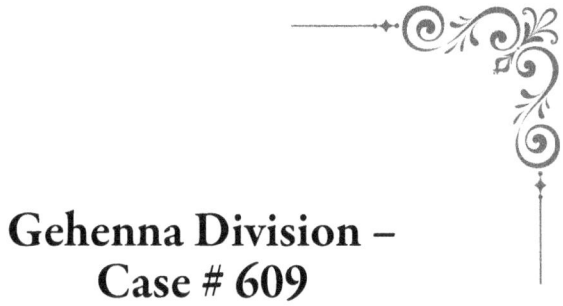

Gehenna Division –
Case # 609

For the last two days, the body of his sister had dangled beside the bed. Long tendrils of ghastly hair swirled around her head and reached down to tickle his bare arm.

Zared Wayward stared past her at the paint-chipped wall. He couldn't bring himself to turn off the bedside lamp. After days of sleep deprivation, his dreams were playing out in the furnished space of his bedroom. He couldn't switch off his visions any longer—Madeline's death was no suicide.

Swinging his legs to the floor, Zared grabbed the manila folder he'd left on the nightstand. The file labeled Gehenna Division, Case #609, shook in his hands. Three years of his life was a small price to pay for the sanctity of a loved one's soul.

So, why was he still holding the file?

Gehenna was a last resort. The only option Zared had left. He would go deep undercover with the new division under the charge of Ezra Knight, the most intimidating person Zared had ever met. Ezra was twice the size of the average man, and his rust-colored horns, etched with bright blue markings, towered over an oblong crown of black hair. His pasty skin stretched tightly over each sharp feature. Almost every visible inch of him had some piercing or elaborate tattoo. But the most disturbing thing about Ezra's demonic look was his black pupils rimmed in fire. Eye tattoos weren't uncommon, but Zared had never seen one with a living, moving flame.

No one in the division knew what Ezra had looked like before the body modifications. Then again, Ezra was a lifer. Zared, however, could come back. He'd be normal again.

What's a few extra surgeries? Whatever they change, they will change back.

A cold hand rested on his shoulder, and Madeline's perfume wafted across his nose as Zared opened the folder. The contract's details sprawled over twenty pages. He glanced over at his sister, the rope still tight around her neck. The scent of flowers turned rancid. Sulfur assaulted his senses as her grey lips twisted and opened in a silent scream. Her soul was being tortured in Hell, and here he was pondering the fine print. As soon as he scrawled his signature across the dotted line, Madeline's ghost vanished.

I'm going to Hell.

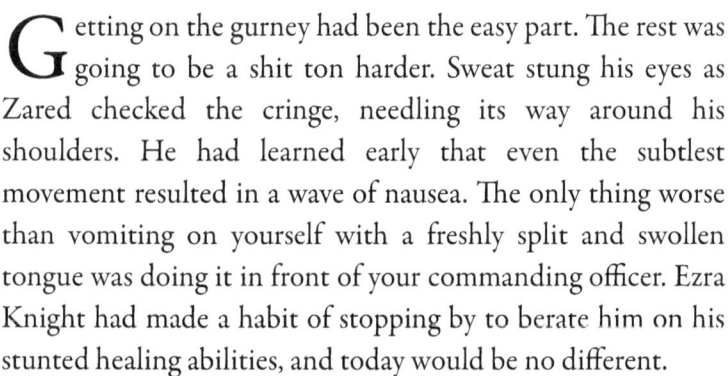

Getting on the gurney had been the easy part. The rest was going to be a shit ton harder. Sweat stung his eyes as Zared checked the cringe, needling its way around his shoulders. He had learned early that even the subtlest movement resulted in a wave of nausea. The only thing worse than vomiting on yourself with a freshly split and swollen tongue was doing it in front of your commanding officer. Ezra Knight had made a habit of stopping by to berate him on his stunted healing abilities, and today would be no different.

Zared leaned across the stainless-steel sink only to recoil

in disgust. The reflection in the mirror wasn't a face he recognized—or wanted—but it was the visage he needed for the job. *Vanity be damned!* Madeline meant more to him than his college-boy good looks. The only identifying mark that remained was the small tattoo on his right shoulder, which was dedicated to their parents after the accident. Madeline had the same one. Zared prayed it would be enough.

"How's it going in there?" The voice on the other side of the door was like a cracking iceberg and held an otherworldly edge. "You're not crying, are you?"

"No, Sir," Zared shouted over his shoulder, still unable to take his eyes off the atrocity before him. His trembling hand flittered over the subdermal implants that ran along the center of his bare skull. Two weeks ago, the head that now had three protruding shark fins was bump-free and covered with silky brown hair. His square masculine jaw had been extended and given a sharp point, his tongue split, and his skin decorated in graphic tattoos and oddly placed piercings. Anger curled his fingers into a tight ball, knuckles turning white from the strain as he slammed his fist into the mirror. The cracks that splintered across the glass only accentuated the monstrosity he'd become, that he had agreed to become to save Madeline's soul.

A gnarled hand opened the bathroom door and tossed a bundle on the floor behind him. "Put these on." Jagged nails scratched the wood as the grisly hand slid the door closed again.

Zared stared at the pile of clothes at his feet. Once the uniform was on, there was no going back. But then, he reminded himself, there was no going back after the hours of painful surgery and recovery he'd undergone. He was a demon now, at least on the outside, one of the Gehenna, an elite law enforcement team transformed and trained to survive the rigors of Hell.

Now, with just over a month of special ops training, he was going into the field. Zared had one arm in the heavy fire-retardant jacket when the bathroom door flew open.

"What's taking so damn long?" Ezra fumed as he stalked to the toilet. He shot Zared a burning glare as he reached for his fly and paused. "What did you do?"

Zared looked down at his clothes, the jacket drooping off one shoulder as he lifted his arms to inspect the uniform. "What?"

The floorboards groaned under Ezra's steel-tipped boots as if he'd suddenly gained a hundred pounds. "Where's Uvall's brand? I clearly stated the upper *right* shoulder."

Unable to handle Ezra's heated stare, Zared slid the rest of the way into the jacket. He mumbled. "It's on my left shoulder."

The geyser of piss that battered the shallow porcelain bowl was almost as threatening as Ezra's raised fist. "Left shoulder! Shit for brains, are you trying to get yourself killed?"

"I couldn't cover up my tattoo. Madeline won't believe me without it." Zared bowed his head. He'd purposely broken protocol for the sake of getting Madeline out of Hell as fast as possible. With the tattoo, he wouldn't have to waste time convincing her of his identity. One look and she'd know without a doubt, but it was a high-stakes gamble to shift the brand. At the time, he thought it would pay off.

"So, you're willing to risk her soul, your life, and possibly mine, all for the sake of a crappy memorial honoring a couple of belligerent drunks? Z, I thought you were sharper than that."

The Waywards might have been deadbeats and their family dysfunctional, but they were all Zared and Madeline had, though not for very long. Zared drilled his superior with a hard look that would have been terrifying had he been a real demon. But for someone like Ezra, Zared's weakness was disgustingly transparent.

Zared took a deep breath and unclenched his fists. He was already on thin ice, and he knew that at no point could he risk losing his cool with Ezra. "I'll keep my arms covered."

"Yeah." Ezra zipped his pants and stabbed the flusher with a single knuckle. "What happens if you screw up down there and someone demands to see your credentials? You can't show them your *left* shoulder. Even the lowest demon is smarter than that."

The Gates of Hell stretched beyond the misty clouds that hovered far above Zared's head. There was no visible end to the thick, towering poles made of shimmering maroon and black scales—the skin of the beast. Lucifer's scales were said to be tougher than iron, impervious to fire, and impenetrable to all weaponry. The Gates were a fortress that only an idiot would enter willingly, Zared told himself, even as he stepped closer and placed his hand on the rough, scaled post. He immediately pulled away as small yellowish blisters sprouted painfully along his palm.

"Put your gloves on," Ezra barked with a shake of his head, and then he turned to dismiss the SWAT team.

Peering inside the gates, Zared noted the narrow stone path lined by high oak trees. A rather peaceful-looking trail led down a steep slope that his human eyes could not follow.

"Where's the staircase?" Zared asked as he pulled on a pair of leather gloves, still keeping a watchful eye on the picturesque scenery of the netherworld. "I heard it was here, too."

Ezra, gazing through the gates, drew up beside him. The flames surrounding his black irises flickered. "Heaven's entrance is directly behind you."

Zared whipped around. Surely Ezra was playing some sort of joke on him. After all, the staircase to Heaven was supposed to be absolute perfection, single floating steps of pristine marble winding brilliantly up into a clear, blue entrance to Heaven. Such a sight could not be missed, but when Zared turned around, the only thing he saw was a pile of crumbled stones in front of a suspended wall of dead vines.

"They deactivated the staircase a year ago."

Zared walked over and brushed his gloved hand over the brittle vines. He watched the small particles float to the ground. "How is that possible?"

"Heaven's an elitist club, now. Unless you're one of the few who have dedicated your life to the church or become disgustingly wealthy to buy a get-out-of-jail-free card, there's no admission."

Zared considered Ezra's words. If what he'd said was true, Madeline would never get into Heaven. She was innocent of the suicide that landed her soul in Hell, but she'd never been *pristine*. She had a rough time after their parents' car accident. She might have slept around a little and developed a few addictive vices, but none of that made her horrible or evil.

Zared rolled his shoulders and spoke through gritted teeth. "Why didn't you tell me...before?"

A slow grin lifted the edges of Ezra's black tinged lips. "Why, Z? Would you have chosen differently if I had?"

"Of course!" Zared said, biting down on the right side of his newly forked tongue, "I can't get her out."

"You can move her from the Seventh Circle into Limbo," Ezra growled. "Madeline doesn't have to suffer for eternity. Instead, she can reside in a pleasant time and place. That's the best any soul can ask for nowadays, to end up in the First Circle of Hell."

"Why haven't people been informed?" Zared asked, turning around to face his superior.

Ezra shrugged his massive shoulders, then tipped his horns in Hell's direction. "You ready to go?"

The crack of the duo's boot heels echoed on the stone path that led through a forest, down a steep hill, and into a quaint town. The buildings, streets, and outlying area looked like any small town in rural America. The people milling about the streets, in various periods of dress marking their time of death, greeted them with downcast eyes as they hurried about their daily business.

This is where Madeline will end up.

Zared took a hard look around. He heard no screams of torture, witnessed no flesh being torn from bone, and he decided it would be enough.

"Over there. That's where we have to go," Ezra said, pointing to the solitary house at the end of Main Street. The red painted sign hanging out front read "Mayor's Office."

The double doors to the mayor's office swung open before the pair reached the front steps. A rich voice bellowed from the dark interior. "Come in, Mr. Knight."

A rolling shiver traveled down Zared's spine as he climbed the wooden stairs and stepped into an empty foyer. The plush carpet beneath his feet swallowed the sound of his entrance. He followed Ezra across the room to a single door, a knocker in the shape of a fist its only adornment. It should have taken six or seven steps to reach the door on the other side of the room, but after five minutes, they remained several steps away, not having moved an inch closer.

Ezra stopped and threw his hand up, signaling Zared to halt. "What's with the games, Neville?"

"Who's that with you?" the disembodied voice rang out. Zared felt the heat of scrutiny even though no one else was in the room with them. "I've not seen *this* one before."

"He's moving up the ranks. Meet Z."

The fist-shaped knocker on the door moved, a bony finger unfolding to point at Zared. "What's your name, demon?"

Zared stifled his immediate response with a grunt. Lower cast demons did not reveal their true identities. In Hell, names had meaning. Names held great power.

"Everyone calls me Z. You should do the same."

The door-knocker's middle finger shot upward and, to ensure the intended insult was seen, stilled for a moment before curling repeatedly, beckoning the pair to enter.

Ezra reached the door first, but he moved aside for Zared. Steeling his nerves with a deep breath, Zared opened the door and walked into a great hall far exceeding the size of the house they had entered. A floral pattern with blooms the color of coal covered each blood-red wall. The floor under his feet shone like a floating oil spill, fluid liquid movement. Above him, a glass roof displayed a night sky even though they had arrived in the middle of the day.

In the center of the vast open space sat a simply constructed wooden desk. Behind it, a plump figure with horns and cloven feet waited. He wore royal garb, an elaborate coat decorated with gemmed cuffs. Atop the desk, to the plump figure's right, was a bloodstained dagger. As Zared and Ezra approached, the demon slipped a hand beneath his jeweled collar and fingered a red and black beaded necklace.

"Why do I have the pleasure of a visit from the Gehenna?" Neville spoke without a single inflection in his voice.

"There's been an infraction in the Seventh," Ezra answered.

Neville pulled the beaded necklace over his bottom lip and slid it back and forth through his partially open mouth. "You don't say. And what would that be, *exactly*?"

A moment of silence passed. Ezra nudged Zared's elbow, but he couldn't find the words to answer while his gaze was transfixed on the demon's necklace. Drops of milky saliva stuck to the red beads but not the black ones.

"The Harpies pilfered a soul into perdition before the case could be brought before the Council," Ezra said with a growl.

"You have proof that this soul was unjustly sentenced?" Boredom oozed from Neville's pores, but he sat straighter in his chair.

"I do," Zared said, finally coming to his senses. He pulled case file #609 from inside his jacket, opened the file to the autopsy report, and tossed it on the demon's desk.

Zared knew the report by heart. The autopsy had proven that Madeline's first vertebra was not dislocated, which usually happens in a suicide by hanging. It also stated that postmortem lividity was found in the buttocks of the body and not in the lower limbs, which indicated Madeline was not dangling. She also had several bruises and scratches—common defense wounds—on her hands, arms, and legs.

"Whoever did this to Madeline Wayward did it to her against her will. And those damn harpies know it," Zared said through clenched teeth.

Neville glanced up from the report, a single brow raised in doubt. "Says here she was a heroin addict. In fact, Ms. Madeline Wayward has many infractions on her record."

Ezra marched up to the desk, the tips of his boots thumping against the wood. "I never said her soul was clean, but her fate is not in the Seventh. We're moving her here."

A groan sounded as Neville leaned back in his chair. "Fine. You have my permission to enter. Travel swiftly and don't get caught. I will not suffer Lucifer's wrath for a weak soul and a *pair* of meddling humans."

Zared ground his teeth to keep from shouting. Ezra had failed to mention that Neville, or anyone, was aware of the undercover work they were doing. Their fate was in the hands of a *demon!* Red sparks impeded his vision, and Zared stumbled as he turned to leave, drawing a sideways glance from Ezra.

The fantasy of Zared ramming his fist through the center of Ezra's repulsive face kept repeating and quickly spiraled until Zared could hold his tongue no longer, "What the fuck was that?"

Ezra stilled and then turned like a Halloween mannequin on a display wheel. "What?"

"They know!" Zared spat. "Hell knows the truth about Gehenna Division."

Bending forward, Ezra flared his nostrils, looking like a bull ready to charge. "Of course, it's *Hell*. Do we have a problem here?"

Zared moved a step back. "Jesus, man! What else haven't you told me?"

Each vertebra of Ezra's spine snapped as he straightened into his seven-foot frame.

A hush settled over them for a long moment. Finally, Zared said, "You failed to mention the closure of Heaven's staircase."

"And?" Ezra said, moving on.

Watching Ezra march toward the door with little regard for his distress only made Zared panic more. He grabbed hold of Ezra's bicep and growled under his breath. "*And* now I find out that we're not *really* undercover, and Hell has full knowledge of our work. This is seriously messed up."

"Yes, this is *seriously* messed up." The clack of cloven hooves echoed through the great hall as Neville moved around his desk and approached the men. "Mr. Knight, your shark-finned rookie isn't going to make it."

Before Zared turned around, his hands fluttered over his head. He'd forgotten the implants were there.

"That's right, Z. You're a demon, a behemoth without emotion, and yet the stench of your virtue is tantalizing. One whiff and the wild imps will fly from their tunnels and caves. They will descend upon you from every portal in Hell and devour your flesh before you reach the Fifth." Neville swiped the line of drool from his mouth.

A heavy weight landed on Zared's shoulder. "Don't worry. I can handle whatever comes at us. We're good," Ezra said, but his words fell on deaf ears.

Shoving Ezra's hand aside, Zared fought against an overwhelming tide of doubt. He paced aimlessly, rubbing the implant that elongated his chin to a sharp point, and wondered how he'd gotten himself into this.

Ezra told me demons are smart. He warned me. So, what am I doing here?

Zared realized he had never truly suffered the pangs of heartbreak until that moment. The pain of his sister's death wasn't nearly as horrific as realizing her flesh would forever remain between the putrid lips of an insatiable beast because he'd failed. Worse, if he couldn't survive past the Fifth Circle, Madeline wouldn't even know he had tried.

A foul odor crawled up Zared's nostrils, interrupting his thoughts. Neville was standing beside him. "Grant me a small taste and I'll transport you to the Seventh and spare you the agony of failure."

"A taste of what?" Zared asked, even though he already knew the answer.

Between Neville's stumpy fingers was the dagger. He pointed the black-stained handle at Zared. "For a piece of your flesh, I will place you in the Seventh, and with that leap, you gain a small chance to rescue Ms. Wayward."

Zared knew he couldn't think about what he was doing. He took the dagger. Removing his left glove, he rotated his bare hand, searching for the best place to start. He decided on the hangnail on his thumb. He slid the thin blade under the cuticle and moved it down, cutting through meat. He sliced the knife to the first knuckle and around, all the way to the bone, like he was peeling an apple. The pain was excruciating, but the only sound Zared made was a single grunt when he finally ripped the flesh away and handed it over to Neville.

The demon slipped the bloody meat between his lips and chewed. Sighing with obvious delight, Neville swallowed and stamped his hoof seven times.

The air was drier and hotter in the Seventh, and a thick coat of white dust covered the barren landscape. In the distance, a lopsided hill rose out of the desolate plain. As Zared moved closer, he realized the small mountain wasn't made of rock and dirt, but human remains. Near the bottom, the brittle bones had been reduced to a baby-fine powder, slowly crushed from the ever-increasing weight piled on top. The bones in the middle of the pile were fragmented, broken, and shattered, but at the peak, the bones were solid skeletons glistening with moisture. Zared knew those bones were fresh.

Ezra walked ahead of Zared, unaffected by the increased temperature and suffocating humidity. Reaching the base of the hill, he plunged his fist into the crumbling bones.

Zared cradled his injured hand and gasped for air. Realizing he was on the verge of heat stroke, he staggered to catch up to Ezra, only to collapse near his feet.

"Ah, this is the good stuff," Ezra said.

Zared closed his eyes and wiped the sweat from his brow. When he opened them again, he could hardly believe what he saw.

Ezra had his hand jammed under his nose, eagerly snorting the calcium dust from his skin. Tilting his head back, he stretched his arms wide. "Best high in Hell, Z."

"What's wrong with you?" Zared scrambled to his feet.

Ezra is a complete lunatic!

"Take me to my sister!" Zared said, cringing as he shoved his injured hand back into the leather glove.

Ezra rubbed a larger bit of bone from his upper lip and walked toward the backside of the hill, waving for Zared to follow.

Soon, a circle of tall pillars came into view. The columns surrounded a large rectangular table. Perched atop each pillar was a long-toothed Harpy. His sister was lying on the stone table wearing nothing but a sheer drape. Her sleek brown hair was splayed over the rough end of the slab. She looked almost peaceful with her arms crossed neatly over her chest. As Zared and Ezra approached, a single Harpy screeched, and Madeline opened her eyes.

Zared ran for the table but didn't make it there in time. He could only watch as the bird-like beasts swooped down on his sister and dug their sharp claws into her flesh. She was awake and screaming when they tore through her midsection and carved out her insides.

In a matter of minutes, they'd reduced his lovely sister to a slick bloodstain and a moist pile of bones. Zared reached the stone table and fell to his knees, a ferocious roar exploding in his ears.

Zared's deafening bellow had scattered the Harpies back to their perches, where they sat patting their bloated bellies and picking leftover strips of meat from between their teeth. He cursed them and went about gathering his sister's bones, but a gnarled hand stopped him.

"This isn't behavior becoming of a demon, crying over the body of a pathetic sinner." A smirk tugged at the corner of Ezra's black lips.

"She doesn't deserve this!" Zared glared and then charged his superior.

Ezra's chuckle was cut short when Zared plowed his shoulder into the giant's gut, throwing all his weight into him. Zared pushed Ezra off his feet and slammed the bigger man's body to the ground. He followed up the assault with a fast right hook. Then Zared smashed the palm of his hand into the bridge of Ezra's sharp nose, which only rekindled Ezra's devilish laughter. *Sick son-of-a-bitch!* Zared cocked his fist to deliver a blow to the bobbing Adam's apple at the top of Ezra's throat—

"Stop!" The familiar voice stilled his arm mid-swing.

A blast to the center of Zared's chest knocked the air from his lungs and left him gasping on his side. Ezra sat up and cracked his knuckles. "Nice job, Fight Club. You just sealed your fate."

Rolling onto his back, Zared coughed to regain his breath. "Madeline?"

A delicate pair of feet moved past his limited line of sight. Zared lifted his head from the dirt. A few feet from him stood his sister, fully intact with not a speck of gore on her despite having been devoured by four harpies.

Madeline tilted her head. "Who are you?" Then she turned her questioning gaze to Ezra. "Is this another trick?"

Zared climbed to his feet and unzipped his jacket. "It's me. Zared."

Madeline raised an eyebrow and huffed, "You are *not* my brother."

"Oh, but he is. Your wish has been granted," Ezra said as he got to his feet and took a dramatic bow.

Zared thought that, along with being insane, Ezra was hammered. But he really didn't give a rat's ass about Ezra's sick addiction to the dust of the dead. His sister was all that mattered. He had to get her out of there. He'd taken a step toward Madeline when she began to retreat. Zared bared his right shoulder.

Madeline gasped and then seized his arm to inspect the tattoo. Running her fingers over the initials of her dead parents, she cried, "What did you do?"

Zared grabbed her in an embrace. Kissing the top of her head, he whispered, "I can't break your soul out of Hell, but I can take you to a better place."

Madeline pulled away. Fat tears trickled down her face. "You shouldn't have come," she said, shaking her head. "Now that you're here, I can't say no."

Missing her touch, Zared reached out. "Say no to what? Come on. We're moving you to Limbo."

Madeline's entire body vibrated. "No!" she screamed. Turning her back on him, she yelled again, pulling clumps of hair from her scalp. "You have to take my place!"

Even through the extreme heat, Zared felt a chill building at the base of his spine. "What?"

"Every sinner is given the option of exchange, the opportunity to trade places with a soul that's cleaner than their own," Ezra said. He slammed his hand down on Zared's shoulder.

Comprehension hit him like an avalanche. Frozen in place, and unable to move or speak, he finally understood. *They tricked me.*

Smoothing the tangles from her hair, Madeline returned to Zared. Her hands were in front of her, fingers intertwined and wringing like a ball of worms. "I'm sorry. You're the only decent person I know. I love you, brother, but I can't do this. You survived Mom and Dad's accident. You're stronger than I am. You'll survive this, too." A smile lifted the corners of Madeline's mouth.

Anger burned in Zared, melting his ice prison. "Have you gone mad?" The question needed no response. Of course, she was crazy. Harpies had just eaten her, he thought, and for the umpteenth time. "We're in Hell! No one survives *Hell.*"

Ezra stretched his massive arms out wide. "Z, the Gehenna is a sham. It's not real—but I am."

All the pieces quickly fell into place. Ezra's unnatural appearance and odd behavior had nothing to do with his sanity and everything to do with him being an actual demon. The folder arriving at his office shortly after Madeline's death, the offer inside to join the Gehenna Division, the training and physical transformation that followed, hadn't been so that he could move around in Hell unnoticed. It was to keep him from ever being able to leave.

Ezra repositioned himself in front of Madeline, his flaming eyes steady on Zared. "One month into your sister's sentence, I came to her with an out, as I do with every new soul. Four weeks is a good breaking point. Long story short, she offered you up as a replacement. And now that you're here, we can make a fair trade."

"A fair trade?" Zared scoffed. "What makes you think I'll go along with any of this?"

A toothy smirk transformed Ezra's grim face. "If you refuse the exchange, your sister goes back on the slab, and you're still stuck here."

"Maybe she deserves her fate," Zared snapped.

A feminine gasp sounded behind Ezra. Zared couldn't see Madeline, but that didn't stop her grief-stricken face from invading his vision.

Rocking back on his heels, Ezra shook his head. "We both know that's not true."

"I shared information on the Gehenna. People know I'm here." Zared was grasping for a lifeline that wasn't there.

"You kept your tattoo. Put the demon brand on the wrong arm. You screwed yourself, Z. Besides, you signed."

The weakness in Zared's knees forced him to the ground. He hadn't read past the second page of the contract.

"Nobody reads the whole thing," Ezra said, crouching beside him.

The most important decision of Zared's life was the one to save his sister's soul. The second most calculated choice he ever made was to keep the tattoo that would identify him as her brother. He never thought those valiant acts would be rewarded with an eternity of torture.

Ezra jabbed a thumb over his shoulder. "Now, will it be you or her on that table?"

Zared leaned forward and eyed the stone slab. A sudden wave of sadness crashed over him, washing away any lingering regrets. Madeline was his sister. He could still save her. "If I take her place, what happens to Madeline?"

Ezra stood and extended his arm to offer Zared a hand up. "I escort her to Limbo, as per the terms of our contract."

It only took a minute for Zared to say goodbye to his sister. Madeline couldn't voice much in return. She'd clung to him, blubbering sentiments of sorrow and admiration, two emotions he knew she was incapable of feeling. But that was okay. Despite the fear and ongoing agony he was about to face, saving her soul from eternal suffering had been the right thing to do.

Zared looked up into a grey, dust-filled sky. Other than the profiles of the fanged Harpies in the four corners of his vision, there was nothing to see, so he waited. He knew it was only a matter of time before the beasts descended upon his body and took their fill. The only thing worse than anticipating the first feast was the last words Ezra spoke before taking his leave.

"See you in thirty days, Zared."

Author Note

Gehenna Division—Case #609 began with a connection I made at a local author conference in 2015. I first met Weldon Burge, a talented publisher, writer, and editor, who was also in attendance. The Creatures Crimes and Creativity Con is an annual writer's conference focusing on mystery, crime, horror, fantasy, and science fiction genres. I was there to speak on author panels, while promoting my previous titles and my newest release at the time, *The Dead Days Journal*.

They say timing is everything, and it certainly was for the creation of this short story. Weldon was assembling the third book in Smart Rhino's successful body horror anthology series, *Zippered Flesh*. This third edition, *Zippered Flesh 3*, was released in 2017. He encouraged me to submit a piece, and although I hadn't ventured into writing that subgenre of horror before, I saw it as a challenge not to be missed. It took several months to craft a story that incorporated body horror, but I finally found inspiration in the tale of a man transforming his appearance into that of a demon to pass through the gates of Hell. While the story leans towards the lighter side of body horror, it still earned a place in a collection that includes works by horror greats like Graham Masterton and the late Jack Ketchum.

Chilling Entertainment tapped *Gehenna Division—Case #609*—for another Simply Scary podcast episode. I signed the media rights contract, but then COVID-19 hit. After that, things got quiet and then went dark—like so many things in life often do.

Death: Through a Cat's Eye

Hours ago, they attempted to pull me away, but she said she liked the feel of my weight against her side. So, that's where I stay until the very end.

My eyes can't release the tears the others cry, but that doesn't mean I'm any less crushed. I love her, too.

The sobs continue as I move from her side to rest my head on her chest. This is a familiar spot. Almost every night of my life, I slept here, listening to the beat of her heart and the soft puffs of air move in and out of her lungs. But everything is quiet beneath my sensitive ear.

Where will I sleep now?

"You need to get Sax in order for them to move her body," the girl who slipped me peanut butter says to *him*.

I dig my claws into the blanket.

He wipes away a falling tear before leaning over with arms open. There's a warning in my eyes, but he's not paying attention. The hands reaching for me never touch my fur.

"Ouch!" He pulls away with a curse and inspects the bloody scratch marks. He turns to me. This time, when he looks, *he* sees. He understands.

"Oh God, she's left us both, hasn't she?" He crumples

beside the bed and lifts her limp hand to his cheek. "What are we going to do, Sax?"

I can't answer the way he does, so I clean the mixture of blood and tears that's dripping down his arm onto hers. The corners of his mouth lift as he gives my head a quick rub.

A clatter of metal and a plod of heavy boots alert me to the people who are about to enter the house. I crouch, pressing my body closer to hers. They're here for her. I hate change, and her leaving will be the worst kind—permanent.

Towering strangers with blank expressions stand in the doorway. They smell funny. There's a loud clank as a hard case drops with a startling boom. Raised voices, urgent cries. There's so much noise. I want to stand my ground, I don't want to leave her, but the commotion is too much. I'm frightened.

I see *him* stand up to address the strangers, and before I realize what's happening, I'm in his arms and he's walking out of the room.

The strangers are going to take her *away*.

I twist and howl until he loses his grip, and then I run and take cover from the chaos. The one I love most is about to disappear forever. She's the only one who truly cares for me. *He* has rules, rules that she has broken for me. Now he'll insist that I stay off the furniture and ban me from sleeping on the bed.

Will he *even remember to feed me with her gone?*

Hours, maybe days, pass before I finally venture out of my hiding spot. There's old food in my bowl, dried-out and crusty. At least he left something. It stinks, bad. The whole house smells different, her scent lingers, but it's not here. Not really.

I hear a soft whimper and move from the kitchen to the living room. It's dark. He's sitting on the couch with his head in his hands. He hurts, too. I don't want to go to him, but I do, because I think she would have wanted me to.

At first, he doesn't notice me sniffing his toes or feel the press of my head against his leg. So, I force a single purr.

"Hey, there you are. Guess you're pretty hungry." He stands and almost trips over me as he stumbles toward the kitchen. I follow. Despite my sorrow, I want food. He scrapes the dish but doesn't clean it. The water in my bowl is stale. It's been there a while, and he doesn't bother to replace it. But fresh food makes my mouth water, and I dig in as soon as the bowl touches the floor.

He leans against the counter, watching me eat. *Is he deciding what to do with me? Will he throw me out?* I eat faster. This could be my last easy meal. No, wait... I should eat slower and bide my time. When I glanced up from my dinner, his eyes were closed. I doubt he's sleeping, but I seize the opportunity. He can't get rid of what he can't see. I hear him call my name as I return to my secret hiding place. I ignore him and curl into myself, warm but alone.

When I emerge the next day, stacks of brown squares line the hallway. Through the dense particles of cardboard, I smell her. Inside are her things. I attack the box, pouncing, scratching, and biting. I create a pile of scraps, but make no progress in freeing her belongings.

I creep through the bedroom door. Her scent is stronger here. I watch as he dumps a drawer full of her clothing on the bed. The stack is too tall, and some items topple over the side onto the floor.

He turns around when I yell at him to stop. "Sax, you want to help?" he says as he replaces the empty drawer and pulls another out. I leap on the bed, climb the teetering pile, and sit boldly on top.

At first, I say nothing, just watch as he swings the drawer around, ready to pour its contents over my head. A fuzzy sock tumbles from the partially upturned drawer before he realizes I'm sitting there. "Hey, what are you doing up here?"

We stared at each other for a moment. Finally, I tilt my head, still trying to translate his meaning. Did "up here" imply to being on the bed or on top of the pile of clothes he's too easily discarding? I don't wait to find out. Grabbing the sock in my mouth, I flee the scene. My new mission is to save whatever I can of hers.

On my fourth trip into the bedroom, the squint of his eyes tells me he's getting suspicious. He stops what he's doing and watches as I casually clean my paws. It's almost as if he's daring me to steal something else. I do.

I grab the closest garment and hightail it out of the room. He chases me until we reach the basement stairs. He pauses, fumbling for the light switch. By the time he finds it, I've already disappeared. His descent down the stairs is slow and methodical as he clicks his tongue and calls "kitty, kitty". She mastered this special call long ago, but he never did. I ignore his attempt to get me out into the open and wait for him to leave my territory.

I sit very still as he moves closer to my hiding spot. He's talking to himself. Something about a tail. He's an idiot. Any time now, he will give up and go back upstairs.

A loud screech echoes, then a shadow falls over me. I scan the area for the cover that once was—*he* moved the couch! I'm totally exposed. I dart to the right and skitter around the corner before he can get his hands on me. For a long second, it's quiet. Then I hear him call my name, "Sax!"

"Oh, come on, kitty, kitty."

Since he's begging, I return but keep my distance in case he tries anything funny.

"Hey, cat, what are you doing with her stuff?" He'll never understand. There's no point in hanging around, so I race up the stairs and quickly search for a new hiding place.

The next day, I'm drawn out by the smell of fresh tuna. Before the idea of a trap registers, I'm in the kitchen gulping down the delectable meat. I know he's there. He's watching me again. It's too late to run, so I eat more. He lets me finish the plate before he scoops me up and carries me into the living room.

Next to the fireplace is a small wooden enclosure. Inside are her things, a pillow, a pair of fuzzy socks, and a soft T-shirt. He's made this...kept her things...just for me.

He places me inside the handmade box and smiles before kneeling. His hands gently stroke my fur from my head to my tail. He wants to soothe me and thinks this offering will make everything better. What's to keep him from tossing the box right out the front door with me in it?

Nothing, that's what!

On the third rub of his hand, I hiss. Claws fully extended, I lash out at his hand and flee back into the basement. I miss his skin on purpose. It's a warning, not an attack. We're not friends. Not yet anyway.

I won't be fooled that easily. He has to earn my trust and love me unconditionally, the same way she did.

.

Author Note

Over the years, *Death: Through a Cat's Eye* has appeared in various pet-related publications and online sites. It is also an intensely personal tale. Any animal lover understands that pets are akin to family, and losing one is a profoundly painful experience. I lost my cat, Maxx, to kidney disease in 2014 when he was just 10 years old. The story occurred to me a few days after we laid Maxx to rest. I returned home from work to find my husband at the dining room table, indulging in a cheesy snack and discreetly wiping a tear from his cheek. This struck me as odd, not because my husband is unfeeling, but because he and Maxx didn't have the best relationship. Maxx was my cat, and Greg was someone Maxx merely tolerated. In truth, Maxx wasn't fond of most people. There are multiple accounts of near attacks and damaged belongings, but let's not speak ill of the dead. What I didn't know was that they had developed a routine just before Maxx got sick. They would share a piece of cheese when Greg got home from work. This touching moment made me ponder how things might have been for Greg and Maxx if I had been the one who had gotten ill and passed away. How would these two have managed without me there to keep the peace? Would they have finally come together as friends or continue to cohabitate as reluctant roommates?

The Corn Maze

Jacey wrestled the end of her tail out of the closed door before turning the lock. She was more than thirty minutes late, thanks to her tail. This was the second time she'd gotten it caught—once in the bathroom door and now in the front door. Not to mention the glass of wine that it toppled. Jacey had considered changing out of the sexy cat costume, but the only other option she had was a wrinkled and torn Dorothy dress. And that outfit was too cliché for a farm turned Halloween haunt.

Why was she rushing to meet friends at a corn maze anyway? She'd rather be almost anywhere else. Flirting with the new bartender at Red Tap was at the top of her list.

I promised Amy.

Settling behind the wheel of her beat-up Honda, Jacey jerked forward to adjust the end of the tail now sharply poking her in the back. She was about to tear the damn thing off when her cell phone rang.

"Where are you?" Amy squealed, obviously unable to hear herself over the heavy-metal rendition of *Monster Mash* blaring in the background.

"Almost there," Jacey said, starting the car.

"Liar."

"It's this stupid tail! I swear it will be the death of me."

"Oh goody, you wore it! Collin will be knocked on his ass."

"Wait, what?" Jacey eased off the accelerator, contemplating making a U-turn.

"Oh yeah, Collin's here with a little redhead."

"So? We broke up months ago. If this is another one of your match-making schemes, I'll just meet you at the bar later."

Amy laughed. "No! We're waiting for you. But hurry, our beer cooler's almost empty."

Twenty minutes later, Jacey turned onto the dirt road leading up to the farm. Several cars lined one side of the driveway. When she spotted Amy's blue Camry, Jacey pulled into the grass field and parked in the nearest open space.

Mindful of her tail, Jacey shut the car door and headed toward the bright lights and rattling hum of generators in the distance.

Rounding the corner, she followed a string of lighted skeletons lining the matted footpath and soon came upon a roughly constructed ticket booth. The overhead sign, torn on one side, billowed in the wind. Behind the plywood counter sat a lonely, rusted stool. She looked around. The hay bales and coolers that made up the concession area were also empty.

There wasn't a soul in sight.

So much for waiting for me...

"Hello? Amy!"

A loud *pop* made Jacey jump.

The generators sputtered, the lights dimmed, and then suddenly everything shut off.

Surrounded by silent darkness, Jacey fumbled through her bag for her phone. Clicking on the flashlight app, she hoped to see Amy standing in front of her—a good scare, well played. But there was no one.

I'm going to kill them.

Without a second thought, Jacey stormed past the ticket counter. She kept the light down to avoid tripping over any unseen obstacles. Her footfalls echoed over the stilled landscape, the crunch of pebbles and dry dirt growing louder with each step.

Where was the laughter, the shouts... where was everyone?

Panning her light to the left, Jacey caught splatters of red over brown stalks. A few more steps and she reached the entrance.

The maze was set up like a demonic cemetery. Styrofoam tombstones and bloody body parts littered the ground leading up to a metal gate. Two large goblin statues stood like sentinels on either side. The gate itself held an array of Halloween decorations—cobwebs, pentagrams, and impaled plastic crows.

Jacey checked the life of her phone battery—forty-five percent. She was hesitant to enter without the overhead spotlights, but decided she wasn't going to chicken out. As she stepped across the threshold, the generators roared back to life.

The maze lit up like a four-acre Christmas tree. Comforted by the restored light, Jacey put her phone away and entered the cornfield.

Once inside, her confidence waned. The overhead lights created long shadows. Some areas of the maze were dark voids. She stumbled twice over the thick power cords that snaked across the narrow trails. The first two turns she made resulted in dead ends. Repeated backtracking and several near falls had her cursing her friends under her breath.

This is officially the worst corn maze ever!

Deeper into the maze, she passed several displays of torture and gore, all obviously fake and commercially gruesome. Then she came upon one so realistic she nearly gagged. A body lay on the ground, its head completely flattened. Somehow, they'd even managed to incorporate the smell of death into the exhibit: a sickening sweet metallic odor.

The biology major in her was perplexed by the thick chunks of bone and brain matter. Jacey leaned over to get a better look. *What materials did they use to make it so lifelike?*

Jacey's fingers were about to grab a piece of bone when she was tackled to the ground and hauled into the stalks of corn. Before she could cry out, a large, calloused hand clamped over her mouth. Her head smashed against the chest of the person who held her tight. She struggled to get away, and then he whispered, "Shhh... It's still out there."

Collin!

After a moment, Jacey relaxed into familiar arms. So, this *was* another one of Amy's elaborate schemes. She should have known. Yet somehow, the way he trembled made her wonder if he was legitimately afraid.

Caught up in the moment, perhaps...

It had been one of the best scares of her life.

A rustling noise came from the right passage of the maze, followed by an odd clucking noise. Like someone was flicking their tongue off the roof of their mouth. Collin stiffened. The clucking grew louder, as did the scraggly scrapes of something being dragged along the dry, cracked ground.

Then Jacey saw the cause—a fully costumed clown.

The long face was covered in white pancake make-up with perfect red triangles painted above and below vacant black eyes. The mouth was wider than normal, and the teeth were strange, thin, and pointy. As the clown moved forward, the cluck-clacking intensified, becoming more guttural. She could see the muscles in its neck working in rhythm to the sound. In the clown's left hand was a large mallet. Not the carnival variety, but the primitive wooden kind that could smash the hell out of someone's head. It was covered in gore.

Collin wasn't the only one shaking now. This was real. The body she almost touched had been alive at some point that night. It was probably still warm. It could have even been one of the friends she was meeting tonight.

After the clown shuffled past, Jacey removed Collin's hand from her mouth. "What happened? Is there anyone left?" she whispered.

A strangled cry sounded close to her ear, and then Collin's arms were crushing around her once more. "Some hid in the barn, but I don't think anyone's still alive."

"We have to get out of here. My car's close," she murmured.

Collin helped Jacey get to her feet. Keeping hold of her hand, he placed his lips to her forehead. "Don't let go."

Jacey shivered as they crept back onto the path that would lead them out of the maze. When they arrived at the entrance, the gate was blocked by a wall of hay bales seven feet high. Collin had pulled Jacey back into the corn to go around the barricade when she stopped him short. Part of a 'Step Here' pad was sticking out from underneath a pile of corn husks. The pad had been purposely moved off the path. Looking around, Jacey pointed to the animatronic ghost that would activate.

One wrong move and they'd give their position away.

Collin sighed and squeezed her hand. At the same time, Jacey felt a slight tug on her costume. Like the tail had snagged against a stalk of corn. *Not again*. Reaching around, she gave the tail a quick yank. The tail didn't release. Instead, it tugged back. Then she was dragged away from Collin.

Jacey shrieked. Twisting and turning, she attempted to break free from the clown. When that didn't work, she tried to anchor herself to the ground. She planted her feet and seized hold of nearby cornstalks, but the killer was too strong and so was that damn tail.

Jacey threw her bag. "Collin, get to the car. Call 9-1-1!"

Collin fumbled his effort to catch the flying purse. The bag upended, spilling its contents. Jacey's car keys landed near his feet, while her cell phone skittered closer to the path. Collin snatched the keys and ran. Jacey lunged for the phone. On hands and knees, she gained some ground. Straining her outstretched arm, she fought against the clown's herculean strength.

Her fingers brushed the edge of the phone. The tip of her middle finger moved it closer. She almost had...

Jacey screamed.

Agony exploded over her hand and sped up to her shoulder. She looked down the length of her arm. A wooden mallet was embedded deep in the earth, where her hand should have been. Jacey's head swayed. Black specs invaded her vision. There'd be no escaping if she passed out now. She bit her bottom lip until she tasted blood.

The clown's whole body shook while making its throaty clacks and clucks, then it bent down and pulled the mallet out of the ground. Jacey rocked forward with another anguished cry. The bloody pile of mush at the end of her arm was unrecognizable as a hand.

There'd be no way to save it. No way to save herself.

Positioning the mallet like a baseball bat, the grisly clown was preparing to swing at her head. The horrid clucking grew louder, faster.

I'm dead!

The mallet rose higher. Her killer flashed a gruesomely wide smile.

Something moved in the corn. A snap.

The clown paused mid-swing. Its smile turned to a sneer as it whipped around.

Collin rushed forward, stabbing a pitchfork through the clown's gut.

As the clown slumped forward, the guttural clucking slowly came to a stop. Pushing the motionless body aside, Collin darted over to Jacey, "Oh my god, are you okay?"

Jacey groaned and then coughed. Her response stuck in her throat. She'd thought he'd abandoned her, but Collin had come back. He'd saved her. Eventually, she found the strength to nod.

"Your hand!" Collin slipped off his shirt and quickly bandaged what was left of her hand. "Let's get you to the hospital."

Collin grabbed Jacey's good arm and threw it over his shoulder, helping her up a second time. Despite the pain, Jacey felt a surge of relief. She glanced over her shoulder one last time to confirm the killer was dead.

A dark shadow moved.

Pulling away from Collin, she turned to get a better look. The shadow was spreading, moving forward. Backpedaling, Jacey realized it wasn't over. She bumped into Collin, her ankle turned, and she fell to the ground hard.

J acey woke to gentle hands caressing her arms, stomach, legs... It felt good. But then a tingling in her arm turned to a stabbing pain and traveled down to her hand. A heavy weight landed on her chest, suffocating her.

She bolted upright. The sun was shining, but she was still in the maze. "Collin!"

"Cluck!"

The clown wasn't dead.

Jacey twisted around. Collin was lying next to her, his head turned to the side. Eyes open, blood trickling from his lips. The pitchfork was buried deep in his bare chest.

"NO!"

"Clack!"

She couldn't see the clown. But she could hear its sinister call. It was so close. Climbing to her feet, she noticed her hand. It was whole again. She also noticed her clothes. Her sexy cat costume had been replaced with a bloodied clown suit.

Jacey screamed.

"Cluck-clack-cluck!"

Author Note

T*he Corn Maze* was born out of my love for Halloween and haunted attractions. It also serves as a heartfelt tribute to the slasher films that formed the backbone of my childhood entertainment. My love for all things macabre took root at a tender age, sparked by a book of poems by the master of horror himself, Edgar Allan Poe, that I read in the company of a pet crow, named Big Fellow. *The Corn Maze* found its place in the spotlight within the October 2017 issue of Suspense Magazine, a strategic decision on my part. I knew this edition would coincide with a review of the *Zippered Flesh 3* anthology, a collection that proudly featured *Gehenna Division – Case #609*. My hope was that readers would delve into both pieces and find themselves ensnared by the eerie worlds I had crafted, much like I had been fascinated by the tales of terror that inspired me. Oh, and to quote some of that review by Amy Lignor, *"The authors that appear in this work are absolutely mind-blowing when it comes to creating thrills, chills and*

skin-crawling moments. In fact, the lot of them deserve whatever award is passed out for short stories that scare the life out of you. There are no bad or boring reads to skip in this collection."

Not bad, huh?

The Uncanny Chronicles

Blaze Sanchez leaned forward in the fraying leather chair, testing the reverb on the sensitive microphone. Despite production objections, he had insisted on using the old mic. The sound was rich and alive. It added something extra to Blaze's voice, a haunting, more captivating depth that could not compare to the wireless mic the studio provided. This interview was a major opportunity for him, the only chance to meet with the highly sought-after Lambert family, who had agreed to only one interview.

Blaze needed every aspect of it to be perfect. Though scheduled as a puff piece, he knew murder and controversy brought the true crime audience and upped the paychecks. This was his make-or-break moment as a reporter vying for the coveted role of permanent host on the wildly popular podcast, *The Uncanny Chronicles*. It was a huge risk to go off script, but regardless, he intended to deliver a scandalous morsel to over a million drooling subscribers.

Tapping his pen on the desk, Blaze watched the sexy new production assistant, Eve, guide the Lamberts to their designated seats. The siblings, all grown and over thirty, slowly made their way to their places. The eldest son was tall and wiry, like a well-worn farmhand. Deep creases marred his forehead and around his narrow brown eyes. The second was the youngest son, a heavy-set man, almost to the point of doughy, with light blue eyes and a loosely trimmed mustache. The last Lambert remained standing rather than taking his seat as he surveyed the studio and flashed a politician's smile at Blaze and the crew. The guy was handsome, and he knew it.

Suddenly, a blonde woman pushed past him, forcing him to take his seat. She was striking in her own right, but she didn't belong. As she sat, Blaze wondered who she was and what she was doing there. While the audio technician leaned in to test each individual's microphone, a sly smile appeared on the woman's full, rust-painted lips.

"Blaze, this is Kristen Hossen. She's the youngest of the Lamberts and will be sitting in on today's interview," Eve announced before throwing a smirk over her shoulder.

This was just the surprise Blaze didn't need. He knew the production assistant purposely kept this important tidbit hidden. She was still pissed over his quick exit after their late-night hookup in the breakroom. It was a cheap shot to throw him off his game. There was no reason for the little sister to be there since the focus would be on the three brothers. Now, he would have to find a way to incorporate her into the conversation.

Taking a deep breath, Blaze composed himself as his production team signaled they were ready to begin. He flashed a friendly smile at the Lambert family, hoping his new veneers would make them feel more at ease, or at least give them a good first impression before they all came to despise him.

"Welcome to *The Uncanny Chronicles*," he said, and then

cleared his throat.

The three brothers greeted him with polite nods, but the sister's smile grew wider, tilted higher on the left side until a slight impression of a dimple appeared. Was she flirting with him? Blaze rolled his shoulders and adjusted the knot on his tie. Under different circumstances, he might have welcomed her to his bed.

Not likely to happen now, not after what he was about to do to her brothers.

"So, we're just going to jump right in and get things started," Blaze announced, trying not to let his unease show as he flipped through his note cards. "Are you all ready to go?"

After another series of nods, the recording light in the corner glowed red.

"Welcome back to another episode of *The Uncanny Chronicles*! Where the stories are too strange to be made up. If you missed last week's show on the Flying Swamp Frogs of Louisiana, you'll find the replay and outtakes on our website, the uncanny chronicles dot com."

"I'm your host, Blaze Sanchez. On today's episode, *A Killer Family*, we are talking with the Lambert family, originally from Albany, New York, and they have a truly uncanny story to tell."

"Welcome, Lamberts!"

"Hello... Hi... Hey."

"Let me start with introductions. First, we have Eddie Lambert, or should I say, Edward Gein Lambert. As you may recall, the Lamberts caused quite a stir among true crime and serial killer fanatics when their full names were exposed in the recent obituary for their dearly departed mother, Lizzie Lambert. Next, we have Johnny Lambert, John Wayne Gacy

Lambert, and Theodore Bundy Lambert, the youngest Lambert. Also, joining us in the studio to lend some support is their sister Kristen Lambert-Hossen.

"I know everyone here is anxious to hear your uncanny story. So, please tell our audience a little about why you're here. Let's start with Eddie."

"Hi. I'm Edward Gein Lambert. My mother's maiden name was Borden, and her first name was Elizabeth, but everyone called her Lizzie. In school, she was teased relentlessly. 'Where's your axe?' and 'Give 'em forty whacks!' That kinda thing."

Blaze stifled a laugh and lifted his hand, a signal for Eddie to pause.

"In case any of our listeners have been living under a rock, Lizzie Borden, a woman from Fall River, Massachusetts, was charged with the 1892 axe murders of her father and stepmother. Borden was taken into custody shortly after the brutal killings, and her trial in 1893 became highly sensationalized by the media. Despite being found not guilty, she was met with suspicion for the remainder of her days. Edward Gein was a notorious serial killer who gained worldwide infamy for his gruesome crimes and served as inspiration for popular books and movies such as *Psycho* and *The Texas Chainsaw Massacre*."

With a sharp nod, Blaze dropped his hand, signaling Eddie to continue.

"Ah, that's right. Mom didn't understand why she was being bullied. Not until she trekked four miles to her town library, where she discovered why. Soon after, she became obsessed with death and then serial killers."

"How did you keep your names hidden for so long?"

Johnny barked out a laugh. "John Wayne Gacy Lambert is a long name. The original JWG, also known as 'the Killer Clown,' was a serial killer and sex offender who raped, tortured, and killed over 30 young men and boys in Illinois. Mom left the Gacy part off the forms when she registered me for school. Kids all thought I was named after a cowboy. Teddy's name almost got out there once, but the school principal made sure the staff never wrote it down or uttered it aloud. As everyone knows, Theodore Bundy was guilty of raping and murdering an unknown number of young women. Can you imagine trying to date girls with that name? My little brother was always Theo or Teddy. There was no need for a middle name. And I was always Johnny. Edward was Eddie. But we weren't necessarily keeping our full names a secret. Just naturally worked out that way."

"So, what was it like growing up?"

Teddy spoke up. "No person grows up the same as another, but we *were* raised differently than most. For example, Mom decorated Johnny's bedroom with clowns. She was always giving him decks of cards and books on magicians. Once, she even gave him a pair of handcuffs and a book about Houdini. Whereas Eddie had a room full of handmade furniture and tools for taxidermy and wood carving. She wanted our likes and interests to be the same as the men we were named for."

"Teddy, how was your room decorated then?"

"I had posters of supermodels, all brunettes, and cars, especially Volkswagens. Mom started handing me college brochures when I was six, which got me interested in college at a young age. Above all, she wanted me to be successful. And I am." Teddy smiled and slid a manicured hand over his perfect hair.

"No doubt about that. For our listeners, Teddy Lambert is the CEO of the trending dating app SparkSync and the newly released ride-share app RideSync. Eddie is an upholsterer and makes high-end wood furniture. Johnny is an event planner and the owner of Epic Events. This proves that their mother gave them more than their names. She molded them into the men they are today."

Blaze turned his attention to their sister. "Kristen, at any point did you feel left out? Did your mom ever reveal or explain who you were named for?"

A soft cough escaped Kristen's lips. "My mother took great pride in naming her children. It was a symbol of defiance against society's norms. Her sons were given names of notorious and reprehensible men, yet they grew up to be honorable and respectable individuals."

Blaze knew a dodge when he heard it. He hadn't been sure how to bring the sister into the conversation, but now that she had openly evaded his question, it was a good time to let the hammer fall. Placing his elbows on the desk, he leaned forward.

"How did your father, Lionel Lambert, feel about the controversial names given to his sons?"

Kristen rolled her rust-colored lips, smudging her perfectly lined lipstick. "Daddy never had much to say about it."

"That's right. Didn't bother him one bit," Eddie deadpanned.

"Your father died when you were a teenager. A farming accident, correct?"

"That's right," Eddie said.

"But the cause of death is listed as undetermined on the

death certificate."

"If you say so, then it must be right," Eddie repeated.

"Eddie, you were with your father that day in the barn. Your closest neighbor heard yelling and reported there was some argument. Can you tell us what happened?"

"Excuse me, what does this have to do with anything?" Kristen said, her brows furrowed. Her arms crossed over her ample chest, which Blaze couldn't help but notice as it heaved.

"Just some family history for our audience, so they can get to know you. It's why you're here, isn't it?"

"Sure is," Eddie said. "And we're getting paid."

"*That's right*, Eddie."

"Daddy fell, is all. He could have hit his head, or it could have been a heart attack. Don't know for sure."

"And what about that neighbor, the one who heard yelling?" Blaze said. "Susan Moore was found dead a few weeks later. No autopsy could be performed due to the condition of her body."

"Yeah, a house fire will do that to you," Johnny answered. "It was the saddest thing. I always liked her. We almost lost our horse barn in that fire. The fire marshal said it was a faulty stove or something. And it wasn't just Ms. Moore who died in the fire. It was also her boyfriend and her stepfather."

"Tragic."

"Life is full of tragedies," Kristen spoke softly, but Blaze heard the warning. She disapproved of his line of questioning. And from the red blotches creeping out from under Teddy's starched collar, he did not approve either.

Over the years, there had been several mysterious deaths surrounding the Lambert family farm, and then later in life, as the sons moved away into their individual lives, more deaths followed. None of the Lamberts were ever charged. Blaze couldn't find anything other than a short police interview with Johnny Lambert on file. A family who had named their sons after serial killers should have raised more questions. Teddy's college roommate. Eddie's first girlfriend. The young man who worked for Johnny's party planning business. Old neighbors, friends, and even their beloved father. Not a single Lambert had been named as a suspect. It was not only improbable, according to some of the officials Blaze spoke to, it should have been impossible.

The recording light blinked twice and then dulled to gray and black. Production was forcing a break. Blazed reshuffled his note cards, making sure to slide the handwritten ones to the bottom of the pile. It was do-or-die time. While the Lambert brothers grumbled and filtered out of the studio, likely to talk about walking out of the interview, Blaze knew he'd either be reprimanded and ordered to stick to the approved note cards or be praised and, in hushed voices, told to keep pressing for answers. He did not expect Kristen Lambert to approach, rust-colored lipstick freshly applied. He pushed back in his leather chair as she perched her hip against the corner of the desk, boxing him in.

"What do you think you're doing? This is not the interview they agreed to," Kristen said, inspecting her perfectly manicured nails.

"I know. It's better. If your brothers want more cash and a book deal, this is how they get it. They're all named after serial killers. You know a 'puff piece' won't cut it. Play along, and we'll get them booked on *The View*. Or Fallon, if that's more their speed."

"You're too ambitious for your own good. Lucky you're cute." Kristen leaned closer. The neckline of her shirt dipped low enough that Blaze could see the black lace of her bra. Even after what he'd done, indirectly accusing her brothers of murder, she continued to flirt with him.

Yeah, he wanted to go there. He was picturing precisely what they could do on his desk when the production assistant slammed a steaming coffee mug down and thrust a folded piece of paper into his face. "Take a look at this. Be ready to roll again in five."

Kristen shifted forward as he unfolded the paper. He held it closer to his body to keep her from seeing. Only two words were written: KEEP GOING.

A smile stretched tightly across his face. He had the green light.

When he looked up, Kristen ran the tip of her index finger over the rim of his coffee mug. "Maybe that's what you want, but you have no idea what they want. Just remember, we can walk anytime. And we have excellent lawyers."

Blaze placed a hand over hers. Her skin was cool to the touch. "I understand you want to protect your family. But this will lead to fame and riches beyond their wildest dreams. Nobody cares about the dead anymore. Victims don't make the news. Killers do. And regardless of what happened or who did or didn't do whatever to whom, your brothers have a unique opportunity here to make a *killing* off their namesakes. Now, are you all in? Or are you out?"

At least he was asking permission. Sort of. He could tell that the sister, though the youngest, played the dominant role in the Lambert family. If he could get her on board with the idea, the brothers would surely follow.

Kristen's eye twitched as she removed her hand from his touch. "I'll talk to my brothers," she said. Quicker than he thought a person could move, she pressed her lips to his, at first delicate, barely brushing before roughly mashing her kiss back and forth. He didn't need a mirror to see that she had smeared her lipstick all over his mouth. He watched her exit the studio, hopefully to convince her brothers to play along.

It was a small price to pay for the story and the chance at a job of a lifetime.

Blaze had wiped his face and was sipping his burnt-tasting coffee when the Lamberts returned to the studio. It took them a lot longer than five minutes. He expected to get some pushback from the brothers, especially Teddy, who had been the most visually reactive to his questioning. Blaze had a mentally concocted rebuttal speech at the ready. But as the Lamberts settled back into their seats, there was nothing but kind words and smiles.

Money talks.

Kristen blew a discreet kiss at Blaze as the audio tech finished with her mic. A few seconds later, they were recording again.

"Let's speak more about tragedy. Of all the tragedies you've faced over the years, and there have been many, which would you say was the most impactful?"

When no one spoke, Blaze addressed Eddie directly. "Would you say it was witnessing your father's death?"

"Yeah, that's right," Eddie answered with a slim smile.

Blaze turned to address Johnny, and the room tilted left.

He shook his head, attempting to ward off a bout of vertigo. "Johnny?"

Johnny rubbed the back of his neck while gazing at the studio's ceiling tiles. "I'd have to say it was the time I saw a dog get hit by a car. Except it didn't die right away. Half of its head was smushed to the pavement while the rest of the body was still trying to run away."

"That's awful. How old were you when that happened?"

"Five, maybe six years old. I can still see it clear as day." Johnny lowered his hand from his neck, clasped his hands together in his lap, and closed his eyes as if to prove his point. "Yup, clear as day."

Before Blaze had a chance to ask, Teddy said. "Seeing my mother on her death bed, slack-jawed, as the life slowly drained from her eyes. That's a permanent stain on your heart and your head. No escaping that."

These were not the answers Blaze was hoping to get. But who was going to suddenly admit murder on a podcast that would air internationally? He had to dig deeper.

Blaze swiped at the beads of sweat that had formed on his brow as silence lingered a beat too long.

"Aren't you going to ask me?" Kristen said.

"Please tell our audience about the most tragic event you ever witnessed."

"I think it might be right now."

"Excuse me?" This wasn't the conversation he had planned for the second half of the segment. And why was his head spinning?

His heart was nearly pounding out of his chest. What was that ringing sound, and why did he taste metal on his tongue?

When he swallowed, it felt like a lump of sand moving painfully down his throat.

"Mr. Sanchez, I believe you are showing signs of distress. Are you having any chest pains? I'm a nurse." Kristen stood, removing her mic as she approached the desk.

Blaze's stomach roiled, and he quickly swallowed the bile creeping up the back of his throat. "Huh?"

"I think you might be experiencing a heart attack," Kristen said.

Blaze watched the studio erupt into chaos as the production team bumbled about and someone shouted, "Call 911!"

Then he felt cold fingertips press down on his wrist. Kristen's lips were so close to his ear that he felt her breath when she spoke. "You spent the last thirty minutes focusing on my brothers and the infamous men they were named after, but you failed to realize that my name means more than all of theirs put together."

Blaze lurched forward, reaching for his chest when he felt his heart constrict suddenly.

"My full name is Kristen Gilbert Lambert-Hossen, and I was named after a former nurse in Northampton, Massachusetts, who was found guilty on four counts of murder and two counts of attempted murder. But her body count was much higher. So many patients at the Veterans Affairs Medical Center died in her care. They referred to her as the 'Angel of Death.'"

With the room spinning and his ears feeling as if they had swelled, Blaze had difficulty processing her words. The pressure on his chest was building. He could barely breathe. But he also knew the old microphone on the desk had picked up every syllable she spoke.

As the studio lights flickered and his vision turned black, Blaze's last thoughts were of the bitter irony that his pursuit of success had led him straight into the clutches of a real-life nightmare, a twisted family legacy that would claim him as its latest victim.

What an uncanny story his death would make.

Author Note

I was inspired to write *The Uncanny Chronicles* after watching the docuseries *Psycho: The Lost Tapes of Ed Gein*. His vacant yet intriguing demeanor, particularly his repeated, detached, and deliberate responses like "That's right" to questions about murder and grave robbing, captivated me. Like many of you, I've always been intrigued by the workings of a serial killer's mind. My interest began with the first book I read on serial killer court cases, *Alone with the Devil* by Ronald Markman. For this long-out-of-print book, it wasn't the killers or the trials that initially sparked my curiosity. It was my father's reaction upon seeing the book's title on my bed during my high school years. He didn't bother with the fine print. He just saw the bold red title and went into a frenzy, fearing I was dabbling in Satanism. I found his reaction hilarious, but he certainly did not. My fascination only grew from there. That's why, if you read any of my books, past or present, you'll come to see that the monster I truly explore most is humanity itself.

The Séance

The dining room was dimly lit by flickering candles, casting moving shadows on the plaster-chipped walls and filling the air with the overpowering scent of incense. The group gathered around a large circular table, their movements slow and hesitant as they prepared for what was to come. Taking their seats, they closed their eyes and clasped hands, connecting with each other in anticipation. A tense silence hung over the room until it was interrupted by creaking floorboards and the ruckus of a chair being moved as the medium took her place at the table.

After a brief pause, Madame Agnes' commanding voice filled the room. "Tonight, we have come together to summon a spirit from beyond. A writer, known for his eloquent words."

This was not the first time this group had gathered to call upon the spirit of Wilson Harker. And their last attempt had ended in tragedy. Madame Agnes knew the death of the first clairvoyant was more likely due to inexperience than the malicious nature of the ghost. The young girl had left herself open too long and didn't have the strength or proper training to channel his rage. However, if Wilson's soul continued to resist moving on, his widow, Elma, was prepared to call on the church for help. But involving them would be a mistake, as they could end up inviting something far worse into the Harker's home. Despite the increasing intensity, Madame Agnes knew the haunting was due to a wrong deed that needed righting. And the longer it took them to discover this wrongdoing, the more violent Wilson Harker's spirit would become. It was their responsibility to discover the source of the offense and resolve it before anyone else got hurt.

Madame Agnes then led the group by asking them to repeat her words. "Wilson Harker, beloved spirit, please move among us and speak through us. We welcome you with open minds and hearts. Show us a sign that you are here."

No physical response was received, but Madame Agnes could feel an intense presence in the room. The chill of its fury was on her neck as electricity ran through her veins. The entity was close, observing them silently.

With determination, she raised her voice. "Wilson Harker, why is your soul troubled? Why do you remain here with us?"

A cold breeze swept through the room, causing goosebumps to appear on exposed skin. Some shuddered, while others gasped as they caught a whiff of smoke. Any doubts about Wilson Harker's presence at that moment should have vanished.

For fifty years, his routine had been the same. After shutting down his laptop and capping his pens, the renowned author would retire to his leather recliner in the corner and smoke two Blackstone cherry cigars.

The medium opened her eyes. "He is here," she said, her voice trembling with a rush of emotion. More eyes opened and heads turned, all anxious to catch a glimpse of their old friend and colleague. Madame Agnes looked around the room, taking note of the people in attendance: Wilson's grieving widow, a long-time friend and editor, two fellow writers, Wilson's sister and her husband, along with an old childhood neighbor, and his ex-therapist. When their eyes and ears captured nothing from beyond the grave, they directed their attention back to her.

"Wilson Harker, I can feel your presence and sense your unrest. Please, give us another sign. Tell us why you still linger."

While the others anxiously waited for another sign from her dead husband, Elma Harker kept her eyes shut tight as she held onto the hands of those around her in fear. Wilson had never scared her in life; he was always kind and gentle. But since his death, he had become a vengeful demon, intent on terrorizing those who entered his home.

Not everyone at the table shared Elma's beliefs. Many tried to explain away the strange events that occurred mostly when she was alone, chalking it up to stress and grief. They could blame bad pipes and an old house for the moans and groans she heard at night. They could even say her fall down the stairs was a stumble or misstep, but Elma knew it was no accident. She had been pushed—no, shoved—while going to answer the door for Wilson's dear friend and editor, Raymond Stanmore. He too, had seen the dark shadow lingering on the stairs and heard the hollow murmurings but, as of late, was reluctant to speak of the incident for fear of being ridiculed.

Elma felt something more sinister was at play, and she no longer spoke of these incidents after being dismissed as tired and distraught. Though it was true that she was grieving and exhausted, it did not explain the horrors she had witnessed in her own home after her husband's passing. She had even gone so far as to invite a clairvoyant to contact Wilson. Six others had witnessed the first séance, with its flickering lights and slamming doors, but it wasn't until everyone had dispersed, everyone except Elma and the psychic, that Wilson revealed himself. A dark, grisly imitation of the man he'd once been. Now something otherworldly and terrible, he'd slammed into the wide-eyed psychic and disappeared beneath her flesh. And while the poor woman had lain wriggling and dying on the floor at Elma's feet, the echo of her husband's laughter rang out.

Ellen Smith continues

Raymond missed the old days, when he and Wilson would meet at this table for scotch and chess. He missed the way Elma playfully scolded them to go to bed when their games stretched on past midnight. He even missed the way she not-so-playfully scolded them for throwing their discarded chess pieces on her highly-polished mahogany table.

Now Raymond clasped Elma's fragile, wrinkled hand and felt the presence of his friend hovering over them. The smell of the incense suddenly turned Raymond's stomach. His head was dizzy with the sweet, heavy aroma.

Raymond wanted to run. He wanted to cry out when Wilson's presence loomed closer still. He could almost hear the rattle of ice in his scotch glass. It took all of Raymond's strength to stay where he was, sitting up straight in his chair.

Elma's hand trembled in his. Raymond gave it a reassuring squeeze.

"We're all here, Wilson," Raymond said, trying to imagine that his friend was here in person and not in spirit. "All the pieces on the board, right? It's your move."

Wilson had been a hell of a chess player. He'd been a literary genius, too. Raymond had known this from the time he'd read Wilson's first book of poetry: *Swiftly Comes The Fall.* It was a masterpiece. Underappreciated in its time, yes, many of the literary greats flew below the radar during their lives. But Wilson had a gift. He had a talent that Raymond had encouraged throughout his life.

The thing about Wilson was that he simply didn't know how to play the game. Metaphorically, that is. In chess, Wilson could plan and execute a ruthless coup. In the literary world, Wilson had never known when to hold back and how to negotiate for more.

That was where Raymond had come in. Raymond was the editor. The salesman. The liaison between raw talent and commercial success.

Raymond had even managed to sell Wilson's last book. It hadn't been easy. For the past year, Wilson had been talking about his latest manuscript, his opus, the masterpiece he'd refused to let Raymond see "until it was finished." When he'd first learned of Wilson's death, Raymond was ashamed that his first thoughts had been of the mysterious manuscript.

Politeness dictated that he focus on comforting Wilson's widow, so Raymond had dedicated himself to Elma. His attention, Raymond noted, had not been unwelcome. Elma had summoned him to the house daily in the wake of Wilson's passing.

However, it hadn't been until a week after the funeral that

Elma sent Raymond to Wilson's home office and begged him to pack it up for her. "I can't bear to look in his desk," she'd sniffled, dabbing away at her ever-present tears. "He never let me see the last book he was working on. He swore he was almost done. Nearly ready to publish."

That was when Raymond found out how long his friend had been on the decline. There was no manuscript. Earlier drafts and proof copies of Wilson's published work, yes. The only new work Raymond found was a drawer with scribbled notes and sketches. There was no rhyme or reason to any of it. It had pained Raymond to see his once-brilliant friend's pages of rambling, barely coherent text.

Nevertheless, Raymond had packaged it up carefully and assured Elma that he would sell Wilson's final work. And sell it he did. Wilson's posthumously published novel, *The Dungeon of Salt and Fury*, had spent over twenty weeks on the New York Times Bestseller list. It had outsold all of Wilson's previous work combined.

No wonder Wilson was refusing to move on to the afterlife. Who could leave behind all that glory?

Or, Raymond thought, glancing down at Elma's hand in his, maybe Wilson was angry about something else entirely.

At Elma's insistence, Raymond had accepted a few select interviews after the successful release of *The Dungeon of Salt and Fury*. Raymond had always been careful to deflect any of the adulation away from himself. "We are listed as co-authors, yes, but the genius was all Wilson's. I'm so grateful that his widow entrusted me to carry out his vision."

And just like that, Raymond had finally been offered a book deal of his own. He demurred, of course, until the furor over *The Dungeon of Salt and Fury* reached a fever pitch. At last, Raymond had accepted a three-book deal, to include a biopic about his life and friendship with Wilson Harker.

That was how you played the game.

If roles were reversed, Raymond thought resentfully, *The Dungeon of Salt and Fury* would never have seen the light of day. The scattered notes that Wilson had left behind were nearly incomprehensible. Poor Wilson. Even in a thousand lifetimes, he would never have been able to sell a book without Raymond to smooth the way. Or, in the case of *The Dungeon of Salt and Fury*, without Raymond to be the ghostwriter.

Wilson had always hated puns. Raymond tried to push the last disloyal thought from his mind, but his stomach still felt like bile. The incense was overpowered now by the scent of Wilson's black cherry cigars. Could Wilson hear Raymond's thoughts? Or could he simply sense the blazing hot guilt that prickled at Raymond's skin?

Raymond gulped, or tried to. The presence of his old friend wavered over his shoulder another moment. Then a dreadful calm passed through him, like Raymond was drowning, like he would suffocate right here at this table, and no one would notice. Elma's eyes were still closed tight. The medium was gazing at the ceiling. Wilson's sister looked nervously at her husband, who yawned. On Elma's other side, Wilson's old friend, Brie, barely disguised an eye roll.

No one noticed Raymond. He gaped like a fish, desperate for air, desperate to choke out a cry for help.

But none came. Raymond was frozen in place, utterly speechless. As if his own voice had been stolen.

D. Lara Smith continues

T*his whole thing is ridiculous.*
        Cue the candlelight, no doubt to hide whatever tricks "Madame" Agnes was going to pull. A money grab from the rich widow.

While everyone else was looking around to see if Wilson's specter had arrived, Brie West scanned the room to see if she could spot any assistants hiding in the shadows or clear strings tied to objects on the table or the table's legs.

Brie jumped when ol' Aggie intoned, "He is here."

We are living a bad B-movie.

And holding hands was so distasteful. Especially since her own were sweating. Profusely. She hoped Elma didn't notice. She desperately needed both hands to fan herself. *Am I having a hot flash?*

A séance, of all things. How many of these would she have to attend to appease Elma? She should change her phone number, show Elma what ghosting really was.

What do I owe the widow? Wilson was my friend for years before Elmas entered the picture.

Not that Elma wasn't nice. After all, she hadn't cut Brie off when Wilson died. No. In fact, she'd allowed Brie into her home, the huge bouquet of flowers obscuring Brie's face when she showed up at the door unannounced, offering additional condolences and a shoulder to cry on post-funeral. "That's what friends are for," she'd offered, and it sounded weak even to her own ears.

Elma had hidden a sniffle behind a fisted hand, taken the proffered bouquet in the other, and welcomed Brie in.

"Please, go make yourself at home in the sitting room while I get these into a vase," she'd said.

And Brie, counting on Elma's distraction with the bouquet, had asked, "May I use the powder room? It was a long drive from downtown."

Elma had waved her in the general direction, before quickly returning her hand to her face to staunch the waterworks that were beginning.

Raymond appeared around the corner, startling Brie so that she jumped. "Brie..."

"Raymond."

Elma seemed to gather herself. "Brie, when you're done, please meet us in the wine cellar. We're going downstairs to toast dear Wilson."

As soon as Elma and Raymond disappeared around the corner, Brie had beelined it to Wilson's study, praying that Elma hadn't put a lock on it. But a mere turn of the doorknob was all that was needed and Brie had access to Wilson's private office. She knew Wilson had kept a lid on a manuscript he'd begun—something completely outside of what he'd written previously and become famous for. He couldn't help bragging to her that what he was working on was his "magnum opus."

She'd wanted to get her hands on it before the dust had settled on his grave. And what better time than the day after an exhausting funeral for the widow?

Brie smiled smugly as she remembered her own cunning. Yes, let the candles flicker and the medium thrash about in her seat and shake the walls, for all Brie cared. Wilson's work was tucked away safe in her own office now. That crap Raymond published as Wilson's last novel was nothing more than some research and his wild mental meanderings.

Thwack.

"Ouch! What did you do that for?" Brie pulled her hand free from Elma's and stared with shock at her, reaching up to rub the back of her head. She'd been smacked so hard, her ears were ringing.

Elma, who appeared to be mirroring Brie's shock, was shaking her head. "Do... do what, Brie?"

"You slapped me!"

"I did no such thing!"

Brie leaned back in her chair to see if Raymond could have done it. But he was not paying attention. A shadow appeared to be coiling along his back. A trick of the light—the crystals in the chandelier above were capturing the flickering candlelight, sending kaleidoscopic prisms around the room.

Raymond's eyes rolled back, and his lips trembled. Then it was Wilson's voice, jagged and hoarse, that spoke to the room. Terrified, Brie retook Elma's hand.

"Imposter. Thief. Betrayer."

The other participants, staring in horror at the trio whose hands locked together so tightly their knuckles shone, slowly got up and moved away from the table.

A deep rumbling moved through the house, and then a great shaking began as the heavy chandelier swung violently. Madame Agnes ushered those standing to the far wall, then turned, prepared to take back control of her séance.

Raymond's body began to levitate up from his chair, his

hand still locked in Elma's, and hers in Brie's, so that they formed a diagonal chain.

"This... is... my... *OPUS*!"

The group members cowered at the unnatural rage they were witnessing.

Everyone but Elma, Raymond, and Brie.

With a reverberating groan, the chandelier plunged to the table, bringing down part of the ceiling and several rafters with it. A startling crack of thunder followed, and the floor gave way, sending the table and the accused plummeting to the stone-floored wine cellar below.

As the room fell silent and dust settled from the ceiling, Madame Agnes cautiously approached the edge of the broken floor and peered over. She let out a piercing scream upon seeing the twisted and broken bodies of Elma, Raymond, and Brie at the bottom. Their hands remained clasped, linked in death as they had been in their treachery.

Wilson Harker's unmistakable, baritone laughter echoed throughout the space.

"Checkmate."

Author Note

T*he Séance* was a collaborative project between friends and seasoned critique partners, each adding their own creative take to the story. The initial concept emerged from the vibrant mind of Ellen Smith, who proposed crafting a short three-part series, designed to captivate and engage audiences through our individual social media platforms. This endeavor was not only an enjoyable venture but also a calculated way to amplify our visibility and reach a wider audience. Our ghostly tale made its debut in 2024, just in time for Halloween.

The project's inception was inspired by a news segment that aired before one of our critique meetings. During that particular CBS Sunday Morning episode, we were captivated by the story of Michael Crichton's widow, who had joined forces with the prolific James Patterson to bring her late husband's unfinished manuscript to life. This intriguing collaboration sparked a lively discussion among us, filled with opinions and insights. Amidst the conversation, a jest was born—a nugget of humor that morphed into a pearl of creative wisdom: "Complete your work, for should you pass from this world, James Patterson might just finish it for you." The thought of such fortune was both amusing and motivating.

But beyond all of that, collaborative writing holds a special place in my heart. It is an art form I hold in the highest regard, as collaborative writing is the cure for the ever-dreaded writer's block! It is a rigorous exercise that hones one's writing prowess, lubricates the gears of creativity, and significantly boosts overall productivity. My passion for this form of writing is so profound that D. Lara Smith and I taught a collaborative writing workshop at the Mid-Atlantic Fiction Writers Institute. Our collaboration in writing has been a testament to our combined vision and dedication, a long-standing partnership. Our joint novel, *Tortured Souls*, is currently in the delicate editing phase, with an anticipated release for the latter part of 2026. The prospect of embarking on more collaborative projects with Ellen Smith excites me immensely, promising new adventures and creative journeys in our shared world of storytelling.

Acknowledgements

F irst and foremost, I wish to express my heartfelt gratitude to the remarkable writers who graciously contributed their work and expertise to this collection, Ellen Smith and D. Lara Smith. Our journey began with what seemed like a simple critique meeting, yet it blossomed into something profoundly meaningful. Our mutual passion for writing, literature, and storytelling forged an unbreakable bond, and it was inevitable that we would become not only friends but collaborative partners. The camaraderie and creativity we share have been nothing short of magical, and I earnestly hope that this shared path continues to unfold for many years to come.

I would also like to extend my gratitude to the many editors, publishers, and devoted readers who have been instrumental in bringing all of these stories to life. Their commitment and belief in my work have been a source of inspiration and motivation, fueling my desire to create.

And last, but by no means least, I am eternally thankful to my husband, Greg, and my family, whose unwavering love

and support have been my anchor through every triumph and
challenge.

Guest Author

Desiree Smith-Daughety (**D. Lara Smith**) was an Honorable Mention recipient in Writer's Digest's 92nd Annual Writing Competition and has been published in various arts and lifestyle publications, including *Up.St.ART Annapolis* magazine, and *Indie Author Magazine*. She has authored two nonfiction books, including *Falcon Guide: Camping Virginia and West Virginia* with Globe Pequot Press, and has edited and ghostwritten nonfiction books. A curriculum manager for an industry-leading education-technology company, she is finalizing her first novel, *The Edge*.

Guest Author

Ellen Smith is a freelance education writer and speculative fiction author. Her published novels include *Reluctant Cassandra* (2015) and the *Time Wrecker Trilogy*: *Every Last Minute* (2017), *Any Second Chance* (2020) and *All Kinds of Time* (forthcoming). Ellen lives with her family near Washington, DC.

Mentions & Websites

Several notable mentions that are worth checking out!

Suspense Magazine/John Raab

suspensemagazine.com

Smart Rhino Publications/Weldon Burge

smartrhino.com

Chilling Entertainment

simplyscarypodcast.com

Desiree Smith-Daughety

dlarasmith.com

Ellen Smith

ellensmithwrites.com

Author

S. R. Webster is the author of psychological thrillers, horror, suspense, and speculative fiction. She is a member of the Horror Writers Association, the Maryland Writers Association, and leads an M.W.A. critique group. S. R. Webster resides with her husband by the peaceful shores of the Chesapeake Bay. When not frolicking in brackish water, she is hard at work on her next novel, *The Weeping House*.

Also, by S. R. Webster

A Girl Named Ghost
Dark Quirks

Upcoming titles mentioned:
The Weeping House
Tortured Souls

Watch for more at srwebsterauthor.com
Or connect on social media

facebook/srwebsterwrites
X/dead_sassy & Insta/sand_e_web

Writing as Sandra R. Campbell

Butterfly Harvest
Dark Migration
The Dead Days Journal

Watch for more at srwebsterauthor.com
Or connect on social media
facebook/butterflyharvest

Want to read more?

The following is an excerpt from the psychological thriller, *A Girl Named Ghost*.

Chapter One
Ghost

The private road leading up to Grandma June's was narrow and winding. Flanked by overgrown vegetation and with no sidewalk or shoulder to walk along, it was not a safe place to wander about. So when I saw a figure dart into the tree line and force its way through a cluster of tangled vines—I knew it was *him*. I had seen the man in the black fedora with the white rose enough in recent days to know he was the one lurking in the woods around Willow Lake.

When the impressive Victorian house came into view, an unfamiliar dread fell upon my shoulders. Returning to my childhood home had never been an issue before. I loved the house where I grew up, even if it looked like something out of a horror movie. And I loved my Grandma June. Bold, feisty, and weird—in all the best ways. There had never been a time when I needed any family other than her.

After parking in one of the designated spots at the end of the stone walkway, I stepped out of the car and rolled my aching shoulders. A gust of wind grabbed my hair, whipping it across my face, temporarily obstructing the view. I hesitated to pull my hair aside. Did I really want to glimpse the hatted man peering out from behind my grandmother's velvet drapes?

I had to remind myself that this was a safe space. It would always be my home. There was no reason to be afraid. I shoved my hair away and forced myself to look up.

In its heyday, the lakeside house had been vibrant and welcoming. A shining star of the Maryland Historical Society, with its steep gabled roofs, decorative woodwork, and tower accented by stained-glass windows. My grandmother had the exterior repainted after my grandfather's death and before I was born. Shades of gray and black purposely transformed the house into a "people deterrent." All that was missing—a silhouette of a mummy in an upstairs window and a flashing vacancy sign in the front yard.

"Was traffic *that* bad?" Grandma June shouted from behind the screen door. Because what other reason would I have to stand and stretch beside my car instead of coming directly inside?

"It's always bad this time of day," I said and went to retrieve the grocery bags from the back of my Infiniti.

"Did you get everything on the list?" Grandma June asked, opening the screen door as I stepped onto the wraparound porch.

Thursday evenings were our weekly dinner and my organic grocery delivery. Not because my grandmother needed it, but because she basked in the attention. Dinner and a glass or two of wine meant a sleepover. Grandma June preferred those visits, so I always packed an overnight bag.

"Everything except for the dirty chocolate herbal tea." I placed a kiss on her cheek and entered the house.

Two words described my grandmother's choice of interior design: ornamental and expensive. Walking into Grandma June's was like being transported to an extravagant antique store, minus the smell of mildew.

Though I knew the only things holding up her priceless works of art were a few rusty nails.

"Darn, I haven't been able to find that tea for months," Grandma June said.

"Have you tried ordering it online?"

"Every site I've been on claims to be out of stock."

"Guess there's an ongoing shortage."

"Nah, I bet some nitwit's hoarding it. Probably Mrs. Duncan over on Kilmer Street. She's the type, you know."

I smiled and shook my head. "No, I don't know."

According to Grandma June, someone somewhere was always plotting mayhem. And once my grandmother got it in her head that *they* were up to no good, there was no convincing her otherwise. "Have you had chocolate tea at her house before?" I asked.

"She's too stingy to offer, but I bet it's her all the same."

Grandma June followed me through the lower level to the kitchen and immediately dove into the grocery bags when I placed them on the granite countertop. The industrial-sized, stainless-steel appliances looked small in the enormous kitchen. Dark quarter-sawn cabinetry was the only feature in this room that revealed the home's actual age. Everything else was modern—shiny and new.

As Grandma June unpacked and inspected groceries, I considered excusing myself to the den to watch the news. Or maybe to go out for a walk around the lake—anything to give us some distance. It would not take long for my grandmother to notice something was bothering me. The longer we were together, the harder it would be to hide the anxiety stewing in my gut.

My need to ask the forbidden question caused the acid in my stomach to rise, while apprehension heated it to a boil. How long would it take for the turmoil to burn a hole through my insides?

In the end, I dropped my overnight bag on the floor and headed for the wine rack in the dining room.

When I returned and set a glass of overpriced cabernet in front of Grandma June, she crossed her arms and leaned against the kitchen counter. For the first time, I noticed she was wearing her favorite blue dress. The one I had picked up at a thrift store years ago for a Halloween costume. The one she confiscated because she said it made her look like Janet Leigh.

"Gigi, it's a little early for wine," she said. "I haven't even put the steaks on yet."

I took a healthy sip from my glass. Today I found it more annoying than usual that my grandmother refused to call me by my given name. Instead, she used the initials of my first and middle names to create something she believed to be more suitable. She also preferred to treat me like a child instead of a twenty-six-year-old adult.

"It's never too early for wine, Gi Ju."

My grandmother sighed before lifting her glass to red-painted lips. She hated it when I referred to her as Gi Ju instead of Grandma June, or even Juniper, in the same way I loathed her use of the nickname Gigi. Unlike her, the oddity of my name—Ghost Grace White—pleased me. After all, it was the only way to honor the mother who had given me life, a name, and nothing else.

"And for the millionth time, call me Ghost."

Grandma June's hands visibly shook as she placed her glass back on the counter without taking a drink. "I will not." With a disgruntled huff, she disappeared into her custom-designed pantry.

Her hatred of my name was one of life's many obscurities.

It was not until kindergarten that I even learned my real name. A teacher's honest mistake when placing name tags on assigned desks had created the first big uproar in my life and resulted in my first argument with my grandmother. After that, I insisted on being called Ghost. Everyone obliged except Grandma June. She had warned me that the use of my legal name would cause me pain. She was right. There was no shortage of cruelty in children, and even in some adults. But I stuck it out and, over time, derived pleasure from the shock people exuded when I told them the reason for my name.

Who else can say they died on the day they were born?

I was about to pour a second glass of wine when my grandmother reappeared, arms laden with bread, potatoes, onions, and a jar of pickled beets.

"Let us enjoy a nice dinner this evening. No talk of sad things. Tell me more about that guy at work. Bishop, is that his name? It's been so long since you've been out on a date."

I watched Grandma June as she began preparing our meal, knowing full well that the conversation we were about to have would not be pleasant. For either of us.

How could I break the heart of the woman who had wiped my tears, kissed my boo-boos, and supported me in every aspect of my life?

How do I tell her that she is no longer enough?

Chapter Two
Juniper

Juniper White tried her best to focus on making Thursday night dinner. Her granddaughter's latest love interest was the only topic she could think of to lighten the gloomy mood descending on her otherwise fabulous home.

"Did I get that right? Is his name Bishop?" Juniper asked again, grabbing a chef's knife and a large Vidalia onion.

"Yeah."

Chop. Chop. Chop.

"Is he good-looking?"

Clink.

"Very."

Chop. Chop. Chop.

"Well, do you like him?"

"Mm-hmm..." The sound of slurping muffled Gigi's response.

Clink.

Realizing she would not get more than a one-word answer or some other noncommittal sound, Juniper let the conversation drop. But every time she heard the *clink* of Gigi's glass on the kitchen table, she turned to see how much wine remained in the bottle. This unwanted distraction led to Juniper nearly chopping off the tip of her finger, twice.

The pinched look on Gigi's face was cause for concern, as there appeared to be more to her dismay than a prickly mood or that Juniper still refused to call her by her full name. She really wished her granddaughter would let that old argument go. There was nothing wrong with the name Gigi. It was a fine name—a name that made sense! Juniper never understood why Gigi willingly tortured herself with the use of *that* name.

The way her granddaughter was drowning her sorrows in a pricey bottle of Silver Oak meant there was something darker and more pressing on Gigi's mind, though there was not much for her to be upset about. Gigi was gorgeous. Blonde and thin. A younger, prettier image of Juniper. Wherever Gigi went, men flocked, though she always kept them at arm's length. Which only confirmed how smart the girl was—and independent, too. Almost to a fault, in Juniper's opinion, with her corporate job and recent purchase of a luxury townhouse. More importantly, she was rich. They both were, thanks to Juniper's late husband, Henry White, who had been rolling in old family money at the time of his unfortunate accident.

May God rest his soul in peace.

The next time Juniper turned her head, Gigi was emptying the rest of the wine into her glass—a distraction that caused Juniper to embed the knife's sharp blade into her middle fingernail, ruining a perfect gel manicure. Juniper set the knife aside and dumped the finely diced onions into the oiled pan heating on the stove. Reaching for a potato to peel, she noticed a tear inching down Gigi's pale cheek. It was not like her granddaughter had been the one chopping the onions.

Juniper could no longer ignore the storm brewing at her kitchen table. She grabbed the glass of wine that Gigi had poured for her and placed it in front of her granddaughter.

"Deary, why don't we talk about it?"

"I'm not sure I can." Gigi's voice trembled. Before she had even finished draining the contents from her glass, she grasped the wine Juniper had offered with her free hand.

"You need to try, because I cannot have you sitting here crying at my kitchen table for no good reason. I've been looking forward to our dinner all week."

"I'm sorry," Gigi said, knuckling a stray tear away. "I don't want to spoil our dinner."

They sat in silence while Gigi gazed out of the bow window over the kitchen sink. The sun had set, so there was little to see on the dark lake. Then, without warning, Gigi shot up from the table, snatched her overnight bag from where she had dropped it earlier, and headed for the main staircase. As a last-minute courtesy, or so Juniper suspected, Gigi yelled down from the first landing, "I'm gonna wash this funk away. Be back in a sec."

Juniper picked up the glass of wine Gigi had abandoned and drank it in a single gulp. She had never seen her granddaughter so untethered. Gigi was all about order and control. She did not get rattled. And she certainly never cried.

M ore than an hour had passed, and there was still no sign of Gigi.

Their Thursday night meal—steak tenderloin with grilled onion, fried potatoes, pickled beets, and fresh bread—had been skillfully prepared, but only a single portion had been consumed.

Juniper hated eating alone. She had just placed a plate of leftovers in the refrigerator when she turned and nearly bumped into her granddaughter, who had emerged out of thin air like an apparition. Juniper cursed under her breath as she clutched her chest. "Goodness, Gigi! I'm too old to be snuck up on."

"Sorry, Grandma, I didn't mean to scare you." When Gigi looked down at the floor, Juniper knew it was not out of shame but to hide the smile pulling at the corners of her granddaughter's mouth. There was no cure for a devious child. Juniper had experienced enough "surprises" over the years to know that Gigi did not mind shocking people. If not by words, then by actions.

"No harm done, deary. Are you hungry?" Juniper said, reaching back into the refrigerator to retrieve the dinner plate.

"Starving." Gigi eyed the empty wineglasses on the table and then wisely poured herself a glass of tap water.

"Well, sit down. I'll warm up your dinner and make you a nice cup of tea."

Gigi wrinkled her nose at the mention of tea and pulled her wet, blonde hair into a ponytail. "Thanks. Are you gonna tell me a bedtime story, too?"

"Don't be a smartass." Juniper knew "smartass" was Gigi's default reaction to kindness.

"Grandma June, I really am sorry about earlier. It's been a rough day."

"Don't fret, deary. We all have them."

Juniper knew Gigi needed something to help her relax and take her mind off her problems. As a loving grandmother, she had just the thing. A unique brew of herbal tea she had developed over the years would ease her granddaughter's worries and give her the best night of sleep

All she had to do was get Gigi to drink it.